# THE UN

Nurse Linda Mannering is regarded as a sensible, down-to-earth and conscientious nurse by her superiors, so she seems the ideal choice to look after the charming and difficult patient Paul Nicholson. But even sensible nurses have hearts . .

# THE UNCERTAIN HEART

BY

SHEILA DOUGLAS

**MILLS & BOON LIMITED**
London · Sydney · Toronto

First published in Great Britain 1982
by Mills & Boon Limited, 15–16 Brook's Mews,
London W1A 1DR

© Sheila Douglas 1982

Australian copyright 1982
Philippine copyright 1982

ISBN 0 263 74025 0

03/0982

Made and printed in Great Britain by
Richard Clay (The Chaucer Press) Ltd
Bungay, Suffolk

# CHAPTER ONE

LINDA Mannering had just finished serving lunch on the children's ward at Queen's College Hospital. She was helping one of the first-year nurses to stack the dishes into the trolley when the telephone rang, and a minute or two later Sister Smith appeared at the door of her office, a frown on her usually pleasant face.

'Staff Nurse! I want to speak to you.' Her voice was sharp and as Linda walked down the ward one of the older boys, a perky youngster nearly ready for discharge, called after her;

'You're for it, Nursie! She sounded just like me mum!'

'Don't be cheeky, Tommy,' the first-year nurse reproved, but Linda only smiled.

She got on well with her young charges and she had no sense of her own importance. It was splendid to see Tommy so lively when he had been admitted two months ago in a deep coma. She reached Sister's office and went in, wondering what she could possibly have done to make the older woman look so annoyed.

'That was Miss Cameron on the phone, Staff Nurse. She's transferring you to Private Block.'

Miss Cameron was the Principal Nursing Officer, whose word was law and with whom there was no arguing. Even so Linda was astonished enough to protest. 'But why, Sister? I love it here, and you're quite satisfied with me ... aren't you?' she ended a little uncertainly.

Sister Smith's face relaxed into a smile as she looked at her young staff nurse. It was years since she had had a girl she liked so much, and it was a pleasure to watch the way she handled the children. Friendly but firm, sensitive to their individual needs, gentle when she needed to be, full of fun with the ones who were getting better. Oh yes, she thought, she was more than satisfied with Staff Nurse Mannering.

'It's only temporary,' she consoled. 'They need someone to special a new admission on the private wing, and they're short-staffed there.'

'So are we, Sister.'

'I know, but we're not very busy at present and Matron knows it.' The old name for the Principal Nursing Officer still slipped out on occasion.

'When am I to start?' Linda asked, resigning herself to the inevitable.

'After lunch. At one-thirty. Which reminds me——' Sister looked through the glass partition at the ward clock—'it's time you went off duty, my dear.' As Linda turned towards the door she added with a smile, 'A lot of the girls would envy you, specialling Paul Nicholson.'

'Paul Nicholson?' Linda repeated. 'Is he someone well known?'

Sister Smith looked surprised. 'Surely you've heard of him?'

'No, I don't think so, at least—who is he?' but before the other woman could answer the telephone rang again, so Linda left the office with her question unanswered.

Paul Nicholson. The name did sound vaguely familiar. On the way down in the lift and as she crossed College Street, Linda tried to recall who the man was. Queen's College Hospital private wing had had more than its share of celebrities over the years—actors, film stars, sportsmen and sportswomen, politicians and society people. It was a fashionable place in which to be ill. Linda had spent a month there last year, but hadn't liked it as much as the public wards. Private patients were often spoilt, difficult and demanding, especially the show business ones.

She arrived at the nurses' dining-room and because she was late, had to be content with sausage and mash and grilled tomatoes. She slid into the last empty place at the big table where the staff nurses sat, and looked around at her friends and colleagues.

'I'm being moved to Private Block, to special someone called Paul Nicholson. Anyone know who he is?'

The other girls stared at her, some surprised, some amused, then Angie Dennison, who was one of her best friends, thumped her on the shoulder.

'Honestly, Linda! We all know you're a bit retarded in spite of that gold medal, but you must have heard of Paul Nicholson!'

'His name does sound familiar,' Linda began cautiously, and the other girls started to laugh.

'It should do,' Angie went on. 'It was in all the papers when he had that bad smash up at Zandvoort in Holland ten days ago. He's a racing driver, you idiot. One of the best. Fast on the tracks and fast off them, if the gossip columnists are to be believed.'

'Oh,' Linda said flatly. 'I don't generally read the gossip columns.' She frowned and stabbed at a dried-up sausage with her fork. 'He'll probably be awful,' she said gloomily. 'Spoilt and conceited. I hate men like that.'

'I'd swap with you any day,' smiled another girl, who was currently on a women's medical ward, and was always complaining that the average age of her patients was around sixty.

'So would I,' Angie said enviously, her pretty, lively face momentarily discontented. 'You meet much more interesting types on the private wing.'

'Celebrities aren't automatically interesting,' Sue Baker cut in. Sue was older than the rest of them, more sensible, less swayed by the glamour of a famous name.

Linda liked and admired her, and wholeheartedly agreed with her.

'The ability to drive a car fast isn't worth much if you think about it.' She took a bite of grilled tomato. 'I'd be more impressed if he'd done something really worthwhile.'

'Like what?' asked Angie.

'Oh . . . like discovering a new wonder drug, or . . . or working for the World Health Organisation,' said Linda, whose older brother was doing just that. She sighed. 'I wonder why they picked *me* to look after him.'

'You've answered your own question,' Angie grinned. 'Because you're not impressed by men like Paul Nicholson. Now I——' she twirled a red curl round one finger and smiled dreamily—'I would just love to special him. I'll bet I could get him to fall for me.'

'He has a hundred girl-friends,' someone remarked, and Angie gave her infectious giggle.

'Then I'd make a hundred and one! Competition always stimulates me.'

Angie wasn't as scatterbrained as she sounded. She was a fine nurse, not given to fooling around on duty. Her talk was more extravagant than her actions. Linda gave her friend an affectionate smile.

'Stick to the medics, love, they're more reliable.' She finished her first course and started on stewed apples and custard. 'I'll bet the private patients aren't having this dreadful food,' but she said it jokingly, for Linda was quite content with her place in the world. She loved her work and didn't have expensive tastes.

The private wing, built between the wars by the Rockefeller Foundation, was newer than the rest of the hospital complex. Smarter too. As you passed through the imposing main doors you were in another world.

The entrance hall was floored in marble, with tall windows and a veritable forest of pot plants. They must have a full-time indoor gardener, thought Linda, smiling to herself at the opulence of it all. There were a few well dressed people around waiting for the lift, but she took the stairs two at a time because the clock in the hall was striking one-thirty and Sister Wheeler, who was in charge of the fourth floor, was a stickler for punctuality.

Linda was out of breath when she knocked on the office door. Sister Wheeler, a formidable figure in crisp navy and shining white, looked pointedly at the old-fashioned watch pinned to her apron.

'One minute late, Staff Nurse.' Her voice was severe. 'And you've been running! Most undignified.'

'Sorry, Sister,' Linda gasped. 'I was working on the children's ward this morning and—and it was rather a rush getting here.' She gave a little half smile which had more charm than she realised.

Sister Wheeler, who remembered Linda from last year, didn't return the smile, but she looked more gracious. 'Nice to have you back, Staff. I was pleased when Miss Cameron told me she was sending you.'

'Really, Sister?' Linda's pretty grey eyes opened wide with surprise. 'I always thought—I mean, I never thought I fitted in especially well here.'

'You're a good nurse, Mannering. And a sensible down-to-earth girl, which is just what I need for this particular patient.'

Sensible and down-to-earth! Was that how people saw her? It sounded very dull.

'And as for not fitting in,' Sister Wheeler continued, 'I don't understand, Staff Nurse.'

Linda tried to explain. 'I'm not really keen on private patients. They're usually more difficult than the ones on the public wards.'

'Private patients are only people!' Sister Wheeler said sharply, with a return to her former manner. 'Sick people, whose needs are exactly the same as everyone else's. Don't forget that, Nurse Mannering.'

'No, Sister.'

'Now about the young man you'll be specialling. He was in a bad car accident ten days ago. They flew him in this morning from Holland—unwisely in my opinion—and in Sir Charles Bonnington's. He has multiple fractures and internal injuries, also quite severe burns.' She opened a folder, put on her spectacles and listed Paul Nicholson's injuries in technical terms. At the conclusion she said quietly, 'It's a miracle that they got him out of the car alive. He's still very ill, but he insisted on coming home—said if he was going to die he preferred to do it in England. A very self-willed young man.' A faint smile touched her mouth. 'Used to getting his own way, Staff. See that he doesn't play you up.'

'I should have thought that with all those injuries he wouldn't be capable of causing trouble,' commented Linda.

'That sort are born to make trouble,' Sister Wheeler stated, rising to her feet.

Linda jumped up quickly and slid back the office door. 'The girls were telling me about him at lunch. Is he really as impossible as he sounds?'

'Depends on your point of view,' Sister returned with a thin smile. 'He's rich, well connected and good-looking. Which could make him difficult to handle, Staff Nurse, wouldn't you agree?'

'He sounds absolutely awful,' Linda said under her breath, matching her tones to the older woman's.

Sister Wheeler had come to a halt outside a pale blue door marked with a nine. 'Awful isn't quite the right word. The young man has a great deal of charm—too much, I'm afraid.' She opened the door quietly and went in, followed by Linda.

The venetian blinds were drawn against the afternoon sun, which was exceptionally strong for September. Linda looked towards the bed, then at the staff nurse who had risen from her chair in the corner.

'Asleep, Sister,' the girl whispered. 'He dropped off soon after that last injection.'

'Good.' Sister Wheeler picked up the patient's chart and studied it with satisfaction. 'Pulse settling again. Temperature still high, though. And his respirations are too fast. Sir Charles is getting the chest surgeon to look at him later this afternoon.'

Sir Charles Bonnington was the orthopaedic consultant, of whom Linda was much in awe—a man of outstanding gifts but uncertain temper. She hoped Sister would still be on duty when he came with his colleague.

'Staff Nurse Mannering will take over now,' announced Sister Wheeler, and the other girl nodded.

'Yes, Sister.' As she followed her superior out of the room she glanced back at Linda. 'Lucky old you,' she murmured. 'I don't know why they couldn't have left me here.'

Marianne Littlewood was an extremely attractive blonde, big-bosomed, small-waisted. Not a girl Linda had ever really liked, though she couldn't have said why. She was mad about men, and inclined to lose her head over them. That was why she was being moved, Linda thought, out of reach of the too attractive Paul Nicholson.

As the door closed she walked quietly across the room and stared down at the sleeping man. She stared for a long time, because he wasn't in the least what she expected. He was good-looking all right, with aquiline features and a firmly moulded mouth. The thing that surprised her was the type of face. Lean and ascetic, it bore an astonishing resemblance to the effigy of a

Crusader which lay in the church in her home village. She was being fanciful, of course. Illness could give that fine-drawn look, and this man had nearly died.

There were ugly bruises on his left temple, and the marks of recently removed stitches near his hairline. Under the fading tan his colour was poor and, as Sister had said, he was breathing too rapidly. There were marks of strain and suffering on the handsome face, even in sleep. She looked at the brown hand flung out on the white bedcover, and her fingers curled gently round his wrist. His pulse was weak but regular. She had been told to chart it quarter-hourly, and to let Sister know if there was any change.

She was still holding Paul Nicholson's wrist when he opened his eyes suddenly and stared up at her.

'Who are *you*?' His voice, though it hadn't much body to it, was clear and attractive. He turned his head slowly on the pillow. 'What's happened to the pretty one?'

'If you mean Staff Nurse Littlewood, I've replaced her,' Linda said quietly, removing her hand and stepping back from the bed.

'Pity,' he murmured, shut his eyes again and drifted off to sleep.

Linda sat down on a chair in the corner of the room. If her patient was going to spend most of his time sleeping she would have to bring something to read. Perhaps she could borrow a magazine later; there were always piles of them on the private wards, discarded by the patients. She missed the busy children's ward and hoped that Paul Nicholson would make rapid progress, so that she could return there soon.

The man was running true to form, she thought wryly. Ill as he was, he had noticed the attractions of Marianne Littlewood, and regretted her departure. 'Pity,' he had said, staring at Linda with those expressive dark eyes.

So by implication he didn't think that *she* was pretty, a fact which shouldn't have rankled but did. Linda had long ago accepted that she was quite ordinary looking— not plain, not pretty. Medium brown hair and grey eyes weren't exactly spectacular. A small straight nose and a clear skin were bonuses, but didn't add up to the devastating charms of redhaired Angie, or the even more obvious ones of Marianne Littlewood. She told herself not to be silly. Paul Nicholson was her patient and that was the extent of their connection. If he wanted Marianne back he could ask Sister for her, and good luck to him!

Linda glanced around the room, noting that it was one of the best ones on this floor—large, pleasantly furnished, and facing—she shifted the venetian blind a fraction to confirm it—towards Regent's Park.

A quarter of an hour passed surprisingly quickly. This time she had to take both pulse and blood pressure. She wound the cuff round Paul Nicholson's upper arm, but however careful she was she couldn't avoid waking him.

He stirred, muttered something and opened his eyes. 'You again,' he murmured, and Linda replied composedly, 'Yes, Mr Nicholson, the pretty one has left.'

The ghost of a grin flickered across his face, as if he remembered their last brief exchange. 'Looks aren't everything,' he commented, and his eyelids drooped again.

What a cheek! Linda thought indignantly, then reminded herself that she had asked for it by her own remark.

He hadn't gone to sleep again, for while she was charting his blood pressure he asked for a drink. She filled the invalid cup with fresh orange juice from a jug by his bed. He wasn't allowed to sit up, so she had to slip a hand behind his head to support him while he drank. The heavy plaster encasing his left arm made him clumsy and his right hand, when he attempted to control the cup for himself, started to shake.

He swore under his breath and pushed it away irritably, spilling a few drops on his hospital gown. He was obviously a man who hated being helpless and dependant on others. Linda mopped the liquid up with a tissue from the bed table and urged him to try again.

'Please let me help you, Mr Nicholson. It's what I'm here for.'

She was still bending over him when the door opened and Sir Charles came in, accompanied by Mr Weston, the chest surgeon. Sister Wheeler was close behind them, so Linda moved back thankfully from the bed, relieved that she didn't have to attend to the two consultants' needs.

Sir Charles looked down at his patient benignly. 'Recovering from the journey, my dear boy? This is Mr Weston, who's going to have a look at your chest.'

Sister Wheeler beckoned Linda forward and the two of them turned down the bedclothes. Quickly and competently they removed Paul Nicholson's hospital gown so that the surgeon could examine his chest. He tapped, listened with his stethoscope, and asked them to shift the patient slightly so that he could listen to the back of the chest, an awkward and painful business which Paul Nicholson endured with gritted teeth. When Mr Weston had finished his examination the two men withdrew with Sister for a discussion, leaving Linda to rearrange the bed.

Even that small amount of activity had left Paul Nicholson exhausted. He lay back against the pillows panting, beads of perspiration on his forehead. Linda wiped them away gently, but he winced as she touched his bruises.

'Sorry,' she murmured, and he smiled up at her.

'It's all right, Nurse.' The dark eyes were very close

to her own. He was lucky, she thought, not to have sustained any serious facial injuries. He could have been badly disfigured, perhaps blinded. Sister Wheeler had said that he had been pulled from the blazing wreck of his car, but only his legs had been burnt, though that was bad enough when combined with multiple fractures, and made nursing him more difficult.

The surgeons came back into the room. 'Well, Paul,' said Sir Charles, 'Mr Weston wants to operate on that chest of yours. He thinks there's some fluid there, which isn't doing you any good. It's making you breathless, keeping your temperature up. The doctors in Holland tried to remove it with a syringe because you weren't fit enough for surgery then, but they had no success. So we feel an operation would be more effective.'

Paul Nicholson shut his eyes and let out a long sigh. It was as if he couldn't face anything more. As if he had reached the limit of his endurance, Linda thought compassionately. Then he opened his eyes again and regarded Mr Weston gravely. 'I won't get better unless you do this?' he asked quietly, and the surgeon shook his head. 'Then I haven't any alternative, have I? When, sir?'

'Tomorrow morning,' Mr Weston told him, 'when you're a little more rested.'

'I'll let James know what's happening, my dear boy,' added Sir Charles. 'Where is he staying?'

'Mr Nicholson's brother left a phone number,' said Sister Wheeler, 'but he'll be in again at five, so you could speak to him if you'll still be in the hospital, sir.'

'Good, good! I'll do that.' Sir Charles laid a large, well kept hand on the patient's shoulder. 'Don't lose heart, lad. We'll soon have you on the mend.'

After they had gone Paul Nicholson lay in silence, staring up at the ceiling, deep in his own thoughts. From the expression on his face they were not happy ones, but Linda didn't interrupt them. What, after all, could she say that would make him feel any better? She returned to her chair until it was time for the next pulse and blood pressure routine.

'Is this nonsense really necessary?' he asked irritably as she wound the cuff round his arm once again.

'It must be, or they wouldn't tell me to do it,' Linda replied gently. 'I know it's maddening to be woken up——'

'I wasn't asleep.' He was silent while she listened with the stethoscope, but when she took the ear-pieces out he spoke again. 'Know anything about this operation they're going to do?'

Only what she had learnt in nursing school, for she had never worked on the Chest Unit. 'Not enough to tell you anything that would help.'

The dark eyes stared up at her, then he smiled faintly. 'Cautious little thing, aren't you?'

'I don't think it's sensible to pretend to be an expert when I'm not. Please, Mr Nicholson, don't worry about it. Mr Weston is one of the top chest surgeons in the country, and this must be quite a small operation compared with the ones you've already had.'

She knew that he had undergone abdominal and orthopaedic surgery in Holland. No wonder he viewed anything further with dismay!

'Point taken,' he said flatly. 'Can I have another drink, please?'

'Would you like some tea? It's gone three.'

While she was preparing it Sister came into the ward kitchen. 'Mr James Nicholson has changed his plans, Staff Nurse. I shall be off duty when he arrives, so I want you to be sure that he doesn't stay too long.'

'Yes, Sister. Are the Nicholsons friends of Sir Charles?' Linda remembered that the surgeon had referred to them both by their first names.

'I believe so. A very nice man, the other Mr Nicholson.'

This was a judgment with which Linda fully agreed when she met him. The orderly came to tell her that he had arrived, so she went along to the office to meet him. James Nicholson looked a good deal older than his brother, in his late thirties perhaps, a big man with a pleasant fresh-complexioned face. He seemed tense and anxious as he enquired how Paul was taking the news that he must have yet another operation.

'Pretty well,' Linda assured him. 'Your brother has plenty of courage.'

'I know that.' The rather heavy face relaxed into a smile as he looked down at her. 'I understand that Charles—Sir Charles Bonnington—wants to talk to me?'

'Yes. I'll get in touch with his secretary. Would you like a few minutes with your brother?'

She led the way to room nine, and watched while James sat down by the bed and laid a large hand over his brother's.

'Rotten luck, old chap,' he said quietly. 'I thought the surgeons had finished with you when you came back to England.'

Paul's eyes looked over the other man's head to Linda, standing just inside the door. 'I have it on the best authority that this is nothing compared with what I've already had done. Don't worry, James, I shall pull through.'

# CHAPTER TWO

THERE were times in the next few days when this confident assertion seemed misplaced. The operation in itself was, as Linda had said, a small one, but Paul Nicholson's poor general condition pulled him down more than his surgeons had expected. He was moved to the Intensive Care Unit, so Linda was allowed to return to the children's ward, on the understanding that she would go back to Private Block when—if—Paul Nicholson did.

On the fifth day after his operation he was transferred from the Intensive Care Unit, and when Linda came on duty at midday he was already installed—paler, even thinner in the face, but no longer breathless, so that she felt his ordeal had most definitely been worthwhile.

He greeted her with a very attractive smile. 'Sister told me you were coming back. I half expected a visit from you in the other place.'

'They don't encourage visitors on the I.C.U.,' Linda explained, 'but I asked my friends there how you were doing. Didn't you get a message from me?'

'No. They probably forgot. They were full up and hectically busy.' He was silent for a moment, then went on slowly, 'I've never seen anything like it. An incredibly hardworking and dedicated lot.'

She looked at him very seriously. 'They did work hard on you, Mr Nicholson, but now you've got to help. Sister says you're being a little difficult over food. You'll mend quicker if you eat the right things.'

He grimaced at her choice of words. 'You make me sound like a machine! I don't have any appetite.'

18

'Talk to the dietician when she comes round tomorrow. She tries very hard to give people what they fancy.'

She had a shrewd idea that from now on he was not going to be an easy patient. Young active men seldom were once they began to recover. Not that he complained when she changed the dressings on his wounds, a tedious and often painful process, or when the physiotherapist put him through his exercises. It was the long hours between when he lay flat on his back, not well enough to read, bored with the television. Then he didn't complain, but he became moody and irritable.

'How can I sleep with that racket going on?' he grumbled one stifling hot afternoon, when the builders were working on the new extension to the outpatients' department. And ten minutes after Linda had shut the window, in an attempt to diminish the maddening noise of the drills, 'For God's sake, Nurse Mannering, do you want to suffocate me?'

It was unusually hot for mid-September, the sort of weather Linda would have welcomed on her holidays, when it had been cool and unsettled. She sighed and did her best to keep calm, for the noise and the heat were getting on her nerves too. After she had reopened the window she went over to the bed and poured him a glass of grapefruit juice.

He drank thirstily and when she was about to move away he stretched out his free hand and caught her by the wrist. 'Sorry, my dear girl. I have no right to take it out on you.' She was aware once again how attractive his smile could be. 'Sit and talk to me. It's impossible to sleep.'

So she sat down, and he stared at her for a few moments before speaking. 'What made you take up nursing? Don't you ever feel like throwing things at your patients? Or are most of them less irritating than me?'

'Some are worse,' Linda said wryly, and he laughed,

then caught his breath, for his chest was still painful.

'Ever regretted taking up this line of work?'

She thought about it quite seriously, then shook her head vigorously. 'No, I love nursing, though when I was at school I wanted to be a doctor like my brother. But my A-level grades weren't high enough, so I did nursing instead.' There was no regret in her voice. She had been deeply disappointed at the time, but had long got over it.

He asked if her father was a doctor and she told him no, that he was a clergyman, rector of the small Shropshire village where she had been born and brought up. She told him about her brother John, at present in Africa working for the World Health Organisation in difficult and often dangerous conditions.

'Some day I want to go abroad, but first I need to learn everything I can about nursing.' She said this dreamily, speaking more to herself than to him, then became selfconscious when she saw how intently he was watching her.

'Don't stop,' he said. 'Tell me more about yourself.'

Her expression was doubtful. 'My life's not very interesting—nothing like as exciting as yours must have been.'

His lips twisted. 'Less exciting but more worthwhile, wouldn't you say, Nurse Mannering?'

This was remarkably similar to the view she had once expressed to her fellow staff nurses, on the day she had first heard about him. Coming from Paul, however, she found it surprising.

'You sound as if you don't care very much for your work, Mr Nicholson.'

He shrugged his one good shoulder. 'The racing's fine. And most of the drivers are decent types. It's the spectators, the mob who watch, the hangers-on—the commercial aspects. Those are the things I detest.'

'Then why do it?' A tactless question and one which she regretted instantly, but he didn't seem to mind.

'Why do it? Because I found I had a natural facility for racing. Speed's like a drug—it gets you and it's hard to give up. It becomes a challenge, then an obsession.' He let out a long sigh. 'I may have no choice after this.'

Linda had learnt from her friends that he had been right at the top of the Grand Prix stakes, one of three drivers still in the running for this year's world championship. It must be a cruel disappointment to be cut down in the middle of a promising career. Perhaps that was why he spoke so sourly about the sport.

'Have you ever watched motor racing?' he asked, and she shook her head.

'Not live. A few minutes on television while I've been waiting for some other programme.' He laughed at her frankness. 'It's not my sort of thing,' she added with a hint of apology. 'I found it absolutely terrifying—all those sinister-looking cars chasing each other round the track, and the drivers . . . so frail, so vulnerable. The human body wasn't built to withstand impacts at high speed.'

'How right you are, Nurse Mannering,' he said drily, and she flushed with embarrassment.

'I shouldn't be talking to you like this. You know more about the risks than I'll ever do.'

That was the only time he talked about himself, although he asked a great many more questions about her background. By the end of the week he knew that her father was a keen student of local history and that her mother was a gifted amateur painter.

'And you, my dear? Do you paint?'

She shook her head with a smile. 'I haven't any artistic talents.'

'None at all? Don't you play any musical instruments?'

'Oh, I play the piano a bit, though I'm not much good.'

He studied her thoughtfully. 'What are you good at, Nurse Mannering?' he asked, smiling faintly.

She shrugged. 'I like to think I'm a good nurse.'

'And what do you do when you're off duty?' The smile grew. 'Go out with the registrar?' She stared at him blankly. 'I mean the young man who sometimes comes in with Sir Charles.'

Linda coloured and shook her head. 'Alan and I aren't interested in each other.'

'You could have fooled me,' Paul murmured. 'He watches you when he should be listening to old Charles.' He laughed, enjoying her confusion.

In fact Linda didn't care for the orthopaedic registrar, a brash young man with quite a reputation among the nurses. 'He looks at all the girls like that,' she said dismissively. 'Do you want a drink, Mr Nicholson?'

'No, thank you, Nurse Mannering. So the young doctor isn't your type? I suppose you have a nice steady boy-friend who spends more time on postgraduate studies than on dating you?'

She shrugged, beginning to be irritated by his bantering manner. 'I don't have a special boy-friend in the hospital. Why should I?'

'Why not? I should have thought some young medic would have snapped you up by now. You should make the perfect doctor's wife.'

He smiled as he said it, but to Linda it sounded somehow like a backhanded compliment. 'What makes you think that?'

'Because you care about your work, my dear girl. And could take an intelligent interest in his.'

'That shows how little you know about the medical profession. Most of them don't want to think about their work when they're off duty. They like gay, lively girls, who make them laugh.' She gave a little sigh as she said this, because one of the young doctors she had referred to had seemed for a short time to be more than just casually interested. For a short time. Then he had got engaged to a dizzy blonde in the records office.

Paul studied her face, which was more expressive than she realised. 'Generalisations are always a mistake. Racing drivers are supposed to be jet-setting playboy types——'

'Like you?' she cut in, glad that he had changed the subject.

He frowned and shifted uncomfortably on his pillows. 'You shouldn't believe everything you read, my girl. The pulp press often gets it wrong.'

She was nettled by the tone of his voice and retorted sharply, 'I have never read one single thing about you, Mr Nicholson. I'm not interested in the gossip columns.'

'Then that makes you a very unusual young woman,' he retorted mockingly. 'And also perhaps a bit of a prig.'

She flushed at his derisive tone, was about to answer hotly but remembered in time that it didn't do to argue with patients. 'I'm sorry you think that,' she said quietly, and rose from the chair by his bed.

For something to do she began to wipe round the washbasin in the corner of the room. He addressed his next remark to her back.

'I'm sorry, my dear, I shouldn't have said that.' She was silent and after a few moments he went on. 'I'm bored and fed up, but that's no excuse for being nasty to you. You're a very nice girl and it was stupid of me to call you a prig.'

'Please drop it,' she mumbled.

He paid no attention. 'You're very sweet. A little too

serious perhaps. You need to fall in love with someone who has a sense of humour!'

She turned round then and met his eyes unwillingly. He was smiling at her with genuine liking, and she knew that she couldn't be annoyed with him for long. Paul Nicholson had great charm when he chose to use it.

'That'll be the day,' she said lightly. 'Would you like tea now?' and that was the end of the conversation.

As the days passed Linda came to realise that Paul was a very reticent man where his own affairs were concerned. Famous racing driver he might be and darling of the gossip columnists, whether he wanted to be or not, but that was his public image. The private man, she felt, might be very different, though in what way she was by no means sure. So when her friends asked her what the notorious Paul Nicholson was really like, she was disappointingly uninformative.

'Nicer than I expected,' which was no sort of an answer, or, 'I suppose he is very good-looking,' at which they threatened to evict her from the common-room.

'I ask you!' Angie exclaimed. 'This girl's nursing one of the most glamorous men in the country and that's all she can say about him!'

It was Sue Baker, with her customary common sense, who told them to shut up. 'You're being very silly. I don't suppose the poor man looks very glamorous— and that's a stupid word for him anyhow—flat on his back, with a drainage tube sticking out of his chest.'

Linda agreed with Sue's remarks. Glamorous was a silly word to apply to Paul. It went with pop stars, show business people. She had already begun to wonder if his reputation for high living might not have been greatly exaggerated by the mass media. The quietly spoken man with the wry sense of humour and an intelligent interest in world affairs didn't seem to fit his newspaper persona.

When she tried to say this Angie sighed. 'Don't spoil our youthful illusions, love. Tell us about his visitors.'

'He's not allowed any, apart from his brother. They seem very close. And his sister-in-law came once when I was off duty. Oh, and his team manager, though he was only allowed to stay a couple of minutes.'

'No girl-friends?'

'Not to visit yet, though Sister says lots of women ring up to enquire how he is.'

'That's better,' Angie said encouragingly. 'He's supposed to be going around with Fenella Freeman. You know ... that model girl. I expect she'll be in to see him when he's better.'

The day after this conversation Linda came back from her tea break to find a woman visitor sitting beside her patient, chair drawn close to the bedside, her hand on top of his. They were talking very intently, and because she came in quietly in case he was asleep, they didn't notice her at first. The woman was youngish, handsome rather than pretty, with good features and dark hair drawn back from her face. Her expression was tender as she looked at Paul.

Linda paused with one hand on the door, wondering whether to leave again, then he looked up and saw her. He smiled, but the woman gave Linda an irritated look.

'Can't we have five minutes' privacy, Nurse? Paul doesn't need anything, do you, darling?' She had a high clear voice, crisp, incisive, used to giving orders. The sort of voice for which Linda didn't care.

'I'm sorry,' she said quietly. 'I didn't know you had a visitor, Mr Nicholson,' and she withdrew to the office.

She asked Sister Wheeler who the woman was. 'Mrs James Nicholson,' Sister informed her. 'Not as pleasant as her husband, is she?'

Mrs Nicholson stayed for another half hour and

called at the office on her way out, to ask for the latest
news on her brother-in-law's condition. 'My husband's
bound to ask me, as he can't get in this evening.'

Linda didn't wait to hear Sister's reply. There were
things to do for her patient. His dressings to be changed,
drugs to be given. She wheeled the metal trolley into his
room and noticed at once that he looked more strained
than usual. Something his sister-in-law had said? He had
seemed quite normal all afternoon. He was quieter too,
and said hardly a word all the time she was attending to
him.

'Aren't you feeling so well, Mr Nicholson?' Linda
asked after a long silence.

He shifted and sighed, watching as she taped the ends
of a dressing securely into place. 'You're very neat,
Nurse Mannering. Why should you think I'm feeling
unwell?'

'You seem ... rather glum. Has something upset
you?' She asked this hesitantly, afraid he might tell her
to mind her own business.

His mouth twisted. He put his good arm behind his
head and stared at the ceiling. 'Not really. I've merely
been confirmed in my belief that most women are
bitches.' He said this with a quiet savagery that shocked
her deeply. When he saw the expression on her face he
laughed. 'Excluding the nursing profession, of course,
and you especially, my dear. I don't believe you have an
ounce of bitchiness in your whole body.'

His eyes ran over her trim figure in its neat blue and
white uniform, and the cynical look was replaced by
one of genuine liking and admiration. 'Sorry, little girl,
I shouldn't be making you suffer, because I'm in a filthy
mood. I seem to have said that before, don't I? Shall we
talk about something else?'

So that was the end of the matter, though it remained
in Linda's mind as a tantalising puzzle. Had he meant

that Mrs Nicholson was a bitch? They had seemed so close, so intimate at that moment when she had come into the room. Or had his sister-in-law told him something about one of his girl-friends that had upset him? It was nothing to do with her anyway, and Linda thought ruefully that she was no better than her friends, indulging in idle speculation about Paul's affairs.

By the end of that week there was plenty to speculate about. Paul's condition showed a sudden and dramatic improvement. He seemed to get stronger every day, so the ban on visitors was lifted and Linda realised just how popular he was. With men as well as women. Several of the top racing drivers called to see him, his chief mechanic, his team manager for a second and longer visit. Most of the conversations Linda overhead could have been in Chinese for all she understood of them.

'What in heaven's name is torque, and why does it matter on corners?' she asked her friends, but they confessed themselves baffled, and she didn't like to ask Paul in case he thought her nosy.

The girl-friends were another matter. It was easy enough to understand them, and Linda derived a certain amount of quiet amusement from their proprietorial ways. They would look her up and down the first time they met her, as if to assess whether she was any sort of a threat.

'They've been reading hospital romances,' Sue smiled, when Linda told her this. 'The sort where the patient falls in love with his nurse!'

'I expect you're right, but I don't think they worry for long.' The two girls were in Linda's room and she was standing in front of her mirror, adjusting her white cap. She peered at her face a little disconsolately. 'Sue, have you ever wished you were beautiful? Not just quite attractive, but really beautiful?'

'I'd be happy if I was quite attractive,' Sue said drily, for she was on the plain side and heavily built. 'What is this, Linda? The girl-friends knocking your self-confidence?'

Linda sighed. 'A bit,' she admitted. 'It must be good for the morale to have men stare after you wherever you go!' She gave a selfconscious smile. 'I'm an idiot, aren't I?'

'Yes,' said her friend candidly, and they both started to laugh.

Linda was rather puzzled by Paul's reaction to the girls who visited him. He seemed pleased to see them, thanked them warmly for coming, would ask Linda to bring a spare cup for tea, but usually heaved a sigh of relief when they went. He did this one day after a dazzling blonde called Mary Lou had departed, leaving an aura of scent and a lipstick on the washbasin.

'Silly kid,' he commented. 'She'll leave her head behind one day.'

'She seemed rather nice,' Linda murmured.

He gave a shrug. 'She's all right, I suppose. Brain like a bird.'

And quite obviously very fond of him, thought Linda, feeling sorry for the beautiful Mary Lou. Perhaps looks weren't enough after all, though they certainly helped.

'You're looking tired, Mr Nicholson,' she commented. 'I think you've had too many visitors today.'

He gave another, more irritable shrug. 'I didn't ask them to come. The only one I really wanted to see was Hugh Mansel.'

Hugh Mansel was his team manager, a quiet serious man who seemed genuinely fond of his star driver.

Linda couldn't help laughing. 'Do you know something? You're thoroughly spoilt! All those gorgeous girls and I don't believe you care whether they come or not.'

His answering smile was wry. 'They're O.K. to take out on the town, but you must admit that their conversation isn't very stimulating. I prefer talking to you, Nurse Mannering!'

She was oddly pleased by his remark, but didn't want to show it. 'They'd be very hurt if they could hear you. Look, if you don't like to put people off, Sister Wheeler will do it for you.'

'I'll bear that in mind,' he nodded, and shortly after Linda left him.

She was off duty that weekend and went home, as she often did. Walking in the garden with her parents on Saturday evening, Linda told them about her new patient, and was astonished by her mother's reaction.

'Paul Nicholson, darling? You're nursing him? How interesting!'

Father and daughter both stared at her. 'You know the young man's name, my dear?' the Reverend Mr Mannering asked.

Linda's mother nodded. 'Of course I know his name, Francis. He's won several races on this year's Grand Prix circuit. They say he might have been world champion but for his accident. Do you think he'll ever race again, Linda?'

'He never talks about it.' Not to her anyhow. Possibly he had discussed the future with his team manager. 'But Mum, how do you know about that sort of thing?'

Mrs Mannering, who never wasted a minute, was dead-heading roses as they strolled along. 'When I was a young girl I was very keen on motor racing,' she confessed, and at Linda's surprised look she added with a smile, 'I wasn't always buried in the country, darling. I was born and brought up in London, remember.'

Linda's father, tall, thin and intellectual-looking, smiled at his daughter across his wife's bent head. 'Your mother never ceases to amaze me, my dear. She's interested in such unexpected things.'

They were darlings, the pair of them, and Linda loved them dearly. Scholar though he was and engaged on writing a book about the Civil War in their part of Shropshire, Mr Mannering was also an excellent rector. And her mother was the perfect clergyman's wife, interested in the parish, energetic and sociable. There were always people in and out of the house, and Linda was never short of young company on a weekend at home, so that she returned to London refreshed and cheerful.

On Monday morning, while she was doing Paul's dressings, she told him how well informed her mother was about him.

'You sound surprised,' he commented drily, and she coloured slightly.

'I never thought of Mum as a racing enthusiast. After all, when they told me I was going to special you I didn't even know——' She broke off in confusion and Paul laughed as she went even redder.

'Who I was, Nurse Mannering? Why should you, my dear girl?'

He was not a conceited man. Linda had already discovered that, and thought it one of the nicer things about him. She smiled a little uncertainly. 'The other nurses knew. They thought I was a bit slow off the mark because I didn't.'

His expression grew cynical. 'You mean they're avid readers of the gossip columns? God, how I loathe journalists!'

'They couldn't write about you if you didn't give them something to build on,' Linda pointed out, and he gave a hard angry laugh.

'Point taken. So what do you suggest? That I never look at another woman? Or enter an enclosed order of monks?'

'Nothing as drastic as that,' Linda answered mildly, aware that she had annoyed him. 'Of course if you settled down and married some nice ordinary girl, that would put paid to the gossip writers.'

'I don't know any nice girls,' Paul growled, caught her eye and gave his wry attractive grin. 'Not well enough to marry, anyhow. Thank God you're back, Nurse Mannering. That sexy blonde was driving me crazy!'

This derogatory remark referred to Marianne Littlewood, who had been standing in for Linda over the weekend, greatly to her delight.

'Nurse Littlewood's extremely efficient,' Linda said firmly, for though she didn't like the other girl, she felt the need to be loyal to her. She was tidying the dressing trolley and was within reach of Paul's hand.

He ran a finger down her bare forearm. 'But I prefer you. You have a quality that's rare in women. You know when to keep quiet.'

He had never touched her like that before, and Linda was suddenly and intensely aware of him as a man. She had always known that he was attractive, but until now she had thought of him only as a patient. Now that he was recovering from his injuries, now that they knew each other so much better, it was more difficult to ignore his physical appeal.

She answered lightly as she pushed the trolley towards the door. 'Well, thanks. It's nice to be appreciated.'

Paul watched as she went out, and she had no way of knowing if he realised the effect he had had on her. An effect that she must take care to avoid in the future. Nurses had to be detached towards their patients. Concerned, yes. Involved in their progress, but not too personally involved. It would be dangerously easy to become as interested in Paul's affairs as some of her friends were. To become interested in *him*.

The close contact between nurse and patient on the private wing could lead to a real intimacy. The bond with someone you had nursed back from near death could be an extremely powerful one, and strictly temporary, Linda reminded herself. Patients were grateful, often effusive in their thanks, told their nurses they would never forget them, but once they had returned to their everyday lives they were gone for ever. It was not unlike a holiday friendship, absorbing while it lasted but brief in the extreme.

She liked Paul for the courage with which he had borne pain and frustration. She liked him for the genuine appreciation he showed towards her and the rest of the medical staff. She laughed at his jokes, but sometimes she found them too unkind for her taste. Yes, there were things about him that she didn't like so much—his contemptuous attitude to many of the women who came to see him, his scorn for many aspects of the sport that had given him fame and success, his worldliness, his cool cynicism.

These less attractive attributes were becoming more obvious as his health improved, though he was always charming to her. So Linda told herself that although she did like him very much, she by no means admired him unreservedly, and felt safer for these thoughts.

Some of this she tried to explain to Sue Baker, when they were having late-night cups of hot chocolate in Sue's room. The older girl had remarked that she was surprised Linda was still on the private wing.

'Does Nicholson really need specialling any more? Aren't you longing to return to the children's ward?'

Linda answered her second question first. 'I suppose I am,' and when Sue stared at this lukewarm reply, 'I've got sort of . . . involved with Paul now. You know how it is when you special someone who's been terribly ill? You want to see it through to the end.'

'Yes, but surely he isn't terribly ill any more? So why are you still with him?'

'I don't honestly know, Sue. I hadn't thought about it.'

'It's obvious that you don't dislike the man as much as you thought you would.' Sue smiled, and it was something about the quality if her smile that made Linda try to explain just how she felt about Paul. The trouble was that she didn't really know. She found herself getting more and more involved, praising his virtues, excusing his faults. 'After all, Sue, no one's perfect——' She broke off suddenly as she saw her friend's amused expression. 'Why are you looking like that? What have I said?'

Sue gave her an affectionate pat on the shoulder. 'Don't mind me. But you're the last person I'd have expected to champion someone like Paul Nicholson.'

'Someone like what?' Linda asked, and Sue shrugged her shoulders.

'Marianne Littlewood was telling us what some of his girl-friends are like—trendy, flashy. You can tell a good deal about a man's character by his women, don't you think?'

'No, I don't.' Linda was quick to leap to Paul's defence. 'They mean nothing. Just—just casual acquaintances. He's so attractive that he's bound to be chased by that sort of woman. They'd drop him tomorrow if he was no longer famous.'

'Who says?'

'Paul says. He said just that only last night. He hasn't much of an opinion of celebrity-hunters.'

'Then he should lead a more circumspect life, and he wouldn't be a celebrity.' Sue leant over the side of the bed on which she was stretched and fished up the evening paper. 'There's a bit about him here. What do you make of that?'

She rustled the pages over, then stabbed with her forefinger at a paragraph in the section headed PEOPLE IN THE NEWS.

'Beautiful brunette Lisa Cantelli flew in from Rome today, ostensibly to discuss her part in the new T.V. series *Air Hostess*. However, a close friend tells me she is more interested in visiting racing driver Paul Nicholson, still in hospital after the Zandvoort smash-up that nearly killed him. The couple were inseparable last year while he was in Italy for the Imola Grand Prix.'

Below was a photograph of Paul and Lisa Cantelli attending some film premiere. Linda studied it in silence and felt a curious pang, that she didn't want to identity. 'Absolute tripe,' she muttered. 'Paul loathes the gossip columnists.' She finished her cocoa quickly and rose from Sue's one comfortable armchair. 'I'm feeling rather tired. I'm for bed.'

'Goodnight, Linda,' Sue said quietly, and as her friend opened the door, she added gently, 'Why don't you ask to be transferred back to the children's ward? I'm sure it would be best.'

# CHAPTER THREE

LINDA didn't try to analyse Sue's last remark, but to some extent she acted on it. At least, she asked Sister Wheeler next morning how much longer she was likely to be on Private Block.

Sister looked vague. 'Until they decide to move you, I suppose.'

'They?'

'Sir Charles will decide some day that Mr Nicholson no longer needs a special nurse. And then Miss Cameron will decide what to do with you.'

'But . . .' Linda stared at the older woman in dismay, 'surely I shall be going back to the children's ward? I want to go back there!'

'Possibly you will, Mannering, but not definitely. Our superiors have their own ideas on these things,' Sister said sourly, for she was frequently at loggerheads with the Principal Nursing Officer.

Put out by this conversation, Linda was less cheerful than usual when she went into Paul's room. She changed his dressings in silence, asked him what he would like for his mid-morning drink and was about to get it when he caught her by the hand.

'Don't do that!' she snapped, and tugged herself free.

He was no longer flat on his back. Propped up by a mound of pillows, he looked less helpless, more in control of his own affairs. He had just taken a newspaper from the bedside table. He put it down again and stared at her very hard, watching as she backed towards the door.

'What the devil is wrong, Nurse Mannering?' he asked

sharply, and the ready colour sprang into her cheeks. 'You've been quite unlike your usual sweet self ever since you came in. And for God's sake what did you think I was going to do just now?'

'Nothing,' she muttered. 'But if Sister came in . . . or the Principal Nursing Officer . . . or anybody . . .' At his unkind laughter her voice tailed away.

His expression became sardonic. 'You'd get into trouble if someone saw me holding your hand? My dear girl!'

The derision in his voice sparked off her temper. 'Everything's a joke to you, isn't it? Your girl-friends, hospital discipline, the nursing profession!'

'If you would just simmer down——' he began.

'But we are told not to be too familiar with the patients. And you make it difficult.'

He flung himself back on the pillows in exasperation. 'Dear heaven, how tired I am of this place!' With one of the quick changes of mood that she was learning to expect, he smiled. 'Come here, Linda.' It was the first time he had called her by her christian name. 'Come here,' he repeated softly, and after a moment's hesitation she approached the bedside.

He took her hand again, holding it firmly so that she couldn't pull away. He gave a little tug, forcing her to sit on the side of the bed. 'No one comes in at this hour. Now tell me, what's wrong? You were upset from the moment you came in. Can't you tell me, Linda?'

Gentle, he was even more devastating than when he was being sarcastic. His thick dark hair, that was always inclined to be unruly, fell forward into his eyes, and he brushed it away impatiently. 'I can't have upset you, but someone else has.'

So Linda told him about the shock Sister Wheeler had dealt her. 'I got the impression she knows I'm not going back. That she couldn't say anything until Miss

Cameron does, but that she was trying to soften the blow.'

Paul studied her thoughtfully, his dark eyes serious for once, his lips compressed. She was acutely conscious of his closeness, of his hard lean body under the blue pyjama jacket. She felt a sudden and alarming urge to lay a hand on his chest, to lean closer, to kiss him on the mouth.

'Are you so dedicated to children's nursing? Don't you like adult patients?'

'I prefer children.' Her voice sounded squeaky to her own ears, and her heart had begun to beat rapidly. 'I must go and get your coffee,' she said breathlessly.

'In a minute. What would you say, Linda, if Sir Charles asked you to go on nursing me after I leave here?'

She was so astonished that she could only stare at him. He let go her hand and relaxed against the pillows with a wry smile. 'The idea doesn't appeal? I suppose that's hardly surprising. I haven't been a particularly easy patient.' After a short silence he added, 'And I've always known that you don't really approve of me.'

To Linda's surprise he sounded as if he regretted that. However, she took him up on his earlier remark. 'You haven't been any worse than lots of other people I've nursed.' She bit her lip, feeling she might have phrased it better. 'But surely you're not ready to leave yet? And where would you go?'

He let out a sigh and stared round the room, with its pleasant but impersonal fittings. 'I shall go crazy if I have to stay in this dump any longer!'

'It's not that bad,' she retorted. 'You should see the side rooms off the public wards. They're half the size and much less attractive.'

He made an impatient gesture. 'I don't need a lecture, my dear girl. I'm well aware that I'm lucky to be here.

But I need a change of surroundings. I haven't spent so long in one place in years.'

She understood and sympathised with the restlessness of a previously active man. 'I do know how you feel. It's not uncommon when patients are beginning to recover. But if Sir Charles thinks it would be all right where would you go?'

'I have friends. Hugh would take me.' Hugh Mansel was his team manager and also a close friend, but looking after a convalescent could create a good many problems for a busy man.

'Why not to your brother?' Surely his nearest relatives were the obvious people, and they seemed very fond of him.

His brows drew together. 'Not to James and Anne.'

'But why ever not?'

He shifted irritably. 'For reasons you know nothing about. So drop it, please, my dear.'

'I'm sorry,' she said stiffly, aware that she had been treading on private ground.

This conversation had given her some idea of what was coming, so that Sir Charles Bonnington's words were less of a surprise than they might have been. He came earlier than usual and pronounced Paul well enough to be discharged, though he seemed to do so with some reluctance. When they had returned to Sister Wheeler's office, he accepted a cup of coffee and thumbed through Paul's notes with an abstracted frown. 'We'll take that arm plaster off before he goes. I'd have liked more union in the left tibia ... mmm ... mmm ... But the boy's desperate to get away from us, and they have a good physiotherapy department at his local hospital.'

'What do you call his local hospital, sir?' asked the registrar.

Sir Charles looked faintly surprised. 'The one near

his home—the old family home in Sussex.'

'You mean his brother's home, Sir Charles?' Sister queried. 'But is it definite that he'll be going there?'

Perhaps Paul had expressed the same reservations to Sister Wheeler as he had done to her, thought Linda.

'Where else should he go?' asked Sir Charles. 'And this young lady will be on hand to keep him up to the mark.' He looked at Linda, standing in the office doorway, his rather severe features relaxing into a rare smile as he studied her earnest young face.

'Me, Sir Charles?' She looked uncertainly at Sister, who said quickly, 'Staff Nurse Mannering has not been asked yet if she's prepared to go.'

'Not asked?' Sir Charles pursed his lips. 'I thought it was all arranged. She will of course be delighted to do so.' He pronounced this with such authority that Linda would not have dared to disagree. She could discuss it with Sister after the great man had gone, for no one could compel her to leave Q.C.H. If she objected Miss Cameron would have to find someone else.

She was still thinking about it when James Nicholson arrived with his wife, and there was further discussion about Paul's departure.

'He hasn't decided where he wants to go?' Sir Charles rumbled. 'Nonsense, my dear James. He either goes to your place or he stays here.'

'You can hardly keep him against his will,' James pointed out with a faint smile, but behind the smile his tension showed through. Paul's curious reluctance to stay in his old home must be hurtful to his brother, thought Linda.

Sir Charles' reply was absolutely typical and amused her very much. 'If he's not prepared to be reasonable then neither am I. I will not have him as my patient unless he follows my advice, and I shall tell him so now.' He stalked out of the office and there was an uneasy silence for a few moments. James looked unhappy, Anne abstracted. Two minutes later Sir Charles returned, smiling broadly.

'Of course the dear boy has seen sense. It's just a question of being tactful.' (Bullying him, more likely, thought Linda.) The surgeon beamed on them all complacently. 'He can leave the day after tomorrow, and Staff Nurse will travel down with him in the ambulance.' Sir Charles waved a large hand in Linda's direction.

She opened her mouth to protest, caught Sister's quick shake of the head and stepped back behind the door. When Sir Charles had gone Sister Wheeler beckoned Linda back into the office.

'I'm sorry he sprang that on you, Staff. Miss Cameron was going to tell you later.'

The Nicholsons were still there, sitting side by side in the small room, sipping Sister Wheeler's excellent coffee. James studied Linda's troubled face, then asked her kindly why she was looking upset.

'Don't you want to come, my dear? We shall be disappointed, though we shall quite understand. Paul can't have been the easiest of patients.'

'No, no!' Linda exclaimed. 'It's not that, Mr Nicholson. I've enjoyed nursing him.' Enjoyed was the wrong word. She took a deep breath and started again. 'I mean, I like him very much, but I prefer ward work. I've never had any ambition to be a private nurse. Sister will tell you . . .' Her words tailed off under Sister's disapproving eye. Conscious that she had been talking too much, she relapsed into an embarrassed silence, which was broken by Mrs Nicholson.

'There you are, darling—I told you she wouldn't want to come. We'll easily find someone through the nursing agency. I'll get on to them straight away.' She finished her coffee and rose, a slim elegant woman with the confident air of someone who always got what she wanted.

She swept past Linda, then turned back impatiently as her husband halted by the girl. 'I wish you would think it over, my dear,' he said. 'We would greatly appreciate your coming. Paul's used to you, and he would take time to adjust to a new nurse.'

He was such a nice man, courteous and kindly. Linda looked up at him unhappily. Was she being inconsiderate, putting her own feelings before those of her patient? 'All right,' she said slowly, 'I will think about it, Mr Nicholson, but I've never done any home nursing, and I don't really know what's involved.'

He patted her shoulder, his expression lightening. 'Nothing you couldn't cope with, I'm sure. Perhaps you'd ring me tomorrow morning?' He felt in his pocket, opened his wallet and handed her a card. 'I'll be at home—there's the number. Telephone me before ten if you can and give me your decision. You do realise Paul isn't quite as well as he thinks he is?'

'Then why are they discharging him?'

'Because he's desperate to get out of hospital. And both Sir Charles and Mr Weston feel that the psychological boost might help, as long as he has good nursing and supervision by our local hospital.'

'James!' Mrs Nicholson's voice was peremptory. 'Do stop badgering the poor girl. It's plain to see she doesn't want to come.' She returned to his side, thrust a hand through his arm and walked him away. As they went she threw a casual remark over her shoulder at Linda. 'I shouldn't bother to ring, Nurse. We'll look for someone else.'

'Well!' Sister Wheeler exclaimed, as the pair disappeared round the bend in the corridor. 'That's one relative I shan't be sorry to see the last of!'

This was so unlike her usual discretion that Linda stared at her, then started to laugh. 'Oh, Sister! She is a bit sharp, isn't she? Shall I not bother to ring, then?'

Sister pursed her lips. 'I should do what Mr Nicholson asked you. He is the relative, not her. I can't think why you didn't say yes on the spot, Staff.'

'Because I'm not sure if I want to do home nursing. I've got the impression that Mrs Nicholson would rather I didn't.'

'Nonsense,' Sister said briskly. 'Why should she care one way or the other? To a society woman of that type a nurse is quite simply a nobody—just someone to look after her brother-in-law, necessary but unimportant.'

'Is that how she sees us?' Linda asked indignantly, and Sister gave a sharp smile.

'You'll learn, Mannering, when you've been as long in this game as I have. Private patients can be extremely difficult.'

'You said before, Sister, that they were just people.'

The older woman's smile disappeared at this remark. 'Medically, Staff Nurse. Socially they're a law unto themselves. And their relatives. Now stop chattering and get on with your work.' She put her spectacles on dismissively and pulled the ward report book towards her.

The Principal Nursing Officer made it plain that while she couldn't order Linda to go to the Nicholsons, she would be very put out if her staff nurse didn't do so. It was a tricky situation and the easiest way out would be to comply. It required quite a lot of courage for Linda to tell Miss Cameron that she wanted to think it over, that James Nicholson had given her until tomorrow morning to make up her mind.

'Mr Nicholson does not have to find a substitute,' Miss Cameron pointed out caustically. 'I should be obliged if you would make up your mind before that.'

'But if I don't go, wouldn't it be up to the Nicholsons to find their own nurse? Mrs Nicholson talked about telephoning an agency.'

'Agencies vary very much in quality,' Miss Cameron commented. 'Sir Charles will insist on one of our nurses. He'll be surprised—no, astounded—if you decide not to go.'

Linda repeated this conversation to her fellow staff nurses over tea. Angie giggled at her friend's remarkably good imitation of Miss Cameron's forbidding manner. 'So she should be astounded, Linda. You must be out of your tiny mind to refuse. One patient to look after instead of a whole ward full!'

'That could be boring,' Sue remarked.

'Not when the patient's a fabulous man like Paul Nicholson,' Angie retorted irrepressibly. 'And the Nicholsons have a super place in East Sussex. A cousin of mine lives in that area and she says it's an old country house with a gorgeous garden. They're rich, Linda, really rich. You'll have a month or two of the high life, so grab the chance with both hands, girl!'

'Perhaps I could suggest you as an alternative,' said Linda, smiling at this extravagant speech.

Angie gave a doleful sigh. 'They wouldn't consider it. The admin staff think I'm too flighty. They wouldn't trust me with a man like that. You are lucky, Linda, to have such a reputation for being sober and sensible!'

Linda smiled to herself, wondering what Angie would say if she knew the true facts—that the chief reason her friend was hesitating was because she was afraid of falling in love with Paul. She had said it now, if only to herself. Previously she had skirted round the issue— avoided the word love, called it plain physical attraction, which it most probably was. Could you love a man of whom you didn't really approve? Of course you could. It happened all the time.

'Hi!' Angie exclaimed, leaning over the table and snapping her fingers in Linda's face. 'You were miles away. What were you thinking about?'

'Trying to make up my mind whether or not to go,' Linda answered, with less than her usual regard for the truth.

The others left soon afterwards, all except Sue, who was off duty like herself. 'Don't get bullied into going if you'd rather not,' the older girl said quietly. 'And don't be pressured by Miss Cameron into making up your mind in a hurry.'

'Good advice,' Linda sighed, 'but it's not an easy decision. They'll be awfully cross if I say no, Miss Cameron and Sir Charles.'

'For a couple of minutes, then they'll forget all about it,' Sue said sensibly. 'We're very small fry in the medical world, love. Never forget that.'

It was a similar remark to the one Sister Wheeler had made, Linda thought ruefully. Were staff nurses that unimportant? They did difficult, useful work. Hadn't Paul said that her job was more worthwhile than his? Comforted by this thought, she went over to the nurses' home, to get ready for an evening out with a small party of young doctors and nurses. It would be a relief to be distracted from her problems for a few hours. She would think about them again when she went to bed.

However, they came back so late that Linda was half asleep as she opened her door, and wholly so almost as soon as her head touched the pillow. She woke in the morning with that uneasy feeling of something disagreeable that had to be done, took a few seconds to remember what it was, then jumped out of bed when she realised the time.

She was off duty until after lunch and it didn't matter that she had missed breakfast, but Mr Nicholson had asked her to telephone him before ten. She showered and dressed quickly, then went down to the call box in the entrance hall, the card with his telephone number on it clutched in her hand. While she was getting ready she had made up her mind. She would tell Mr Nicholson that she was very sorry, but she would prefer not to nurse his brother any more. What Miss Cameron would say she preferred not to think about.

She dialled the number, waited and pressed some ten-pence coins into the slot. 'Hallo. May I speak to Mr Nicholson, please?'

It was a woman's voice the other end, but not Mrs Nicholson's. When James came on the line he sounded anxious. 'Nurse Mannering? Good of you to ring so promptly. I hope you've decided to come?'

On the telephone his voice was remarkably like Paul's. He was going to be very disappointed when she told him her decision. 'Yes, Mr Nicholson, I've decided.' She hesitated, finding it difficult to say the words, which was ridiculous when he was such an agreeable, gentle man. He wouldn't snap as Miss Cameron might. 'I've decided——' she swallowed and then found herself saying the exact opposite of what she had intended—'that I'd like to come very much.'

He let out a relieved sigh. 'I'm so glad. I was afraid you wouldn't. And Paul will be delighted too. Have you told him yet?'

'No, because I shan't be seeing him until after midday.'

'Then I shall ring him up. Goodbye, my dear—until tomorrow. We shall do our best to make your stay a pleasant one.'

When she had put the telephone down Linda went to the staff canteen, where one could get a cup of coffee at any hour of the day or night. What had got into her to make her change her mind at the last moment? It was disagreeable disappointing people, but surely she could have extricated herself gracefully? The truth was that half of her wanted to go, though she was unwilling to admit it. It was not fear of her superiors' disapproval that had led to her decision; it was reluctance to say goodbye to Paul.

Miss Cameron behaved as if Linda's decision had never been in doubt. Sister Wheeler said sourly that the Principal Nursing Officer had no idea what real life was like. Where did she think a replacement was coming from if Linda went off at five?

'I'll stop if you can't manage, Sister. I shan't have a lot of packing to do.'

Miss Cameron had made it plain that Linda was to wear her Queen's uniform except when she was off duty. 'You are still one of our nurses, never forget that.'

Sister Wheeler smiled faintly and said that she supposed she would manage somehow. 'The young man doesn't need so much attention now. Well, off you go, Staff, and tell him the good news. He was afraid you didn't intend to go.'

This was flattering if true, but had the effect of making Linda feel shy. When she opened the door of Paul's room, he was sitting in the easy chair by the window with his plastered leg on a footstool. He smiled at her warmly.

'James told me you're coming. I hope they didn't twist your arm over it?'

She shut the door slowly, trying to school her face so that she shouldn't give too much away. 'No one twisted my arm,' she said lightly. 'My friends all encouraged me to accept. They say I'm going to have an easy time in pleasant surroundings.' She looked at him then, and in spite of herself she started to smile. It was idiotic, but once started she couldn't stop. She felt relieved, happy, excited at the prospect. 'The other girls will envy me,' she added idiotically.

He laughed. 'That's because they don't know what I can be like. What made you change your mind?'

'We—ell,' she eyed him doubtfully, 'your brother

seemed so disappointed when he thought I was going to say no.'

'And didn't my feelings carry any weight?' he teased.

She looked out of the window, and noticed that the trees in Regent's Park were beginning to change colour. 'Angie—one of my friends—says your brother has a lovely place. It should be nice at this time of year, shouldn't it?'

'Very nice,' he agreed. 'But you haven't answered my question, Nurse Mannering.'

'Because I didn't want to offend you, Mr Nicholson!' She matched her tone to his, making a joke of it, anxious to keep it light.

He had different ideas, however. His expression sobered. He looked unusually serious, then he said quietly, 'I should have hated someone else, Linda. I don't even like it when you're off duty. Thank you for agreeing to come.'

# CHAPTER FOUR

THEY left Queen's College Hospital at nine o'clock on the following morning. As the ambulance turned into the Marylebone Road, Linda looked back at the familiar red brick buildings, which had been her only place of work until now. The sense of excitement was still with her, of being on the brink of a whole new way of life. Conscious that she was being fanciful, she looked at Paul, whom they had decided to transport lying down, in case of jarring to his fractured legs.

He smiled at her. 'No second thoughts about coming?'

'None,' she said gaily. 'It's a beautiful day, just right for a trip into the country.'

'And Faversham looks its best in the autumn. The trees in the park are quite something.' He was silent a moment, frowning slightly. 'There were times when I never expected to see it again.'

Linda was sitting beside him. Impulsively she leant forward and squeezed his hand. 'There were times when none of us were sure you were going to make it. Oh, Paul, I'm so glad you're better!' Then she recalled Sister Wheeler's disapproving look when she had once before used his first name, and bit her lip. 'I'm sorry, Mr Nicholson.' She took her hand away quickly.

His lips twitched. 'My dear girl, we're not in Q.C.H. now. Feel free to call me Paul.'

'Should I?' she asked doubtfully, remembering Miss Cameron's insistence that she must maintain the high standards of Queen's nurses.

'Oh, for God's sake, Linda!' he exclaimed irritably.

'Don't be such a little idiot! Are you completely dominated by rules and regulations?'

'No, I'm not,' she countered with spirit, 'but hospital life is a bit like the army. You need regulations for things to run smoothly. In an emergency someone has to give orders and someone has to obey them.'

The attractive smile, that she found so difficult to resist, transformed his face. 'Sorry, Staff Nurse,' he said solemnly. 'You're right as usual and I'm wrong. But in private, when no one else is around, could you bring yourself to call me Paul?'

The journey took longer than expected, because of the heavy traffic on the outskirts of London. They left the A21 near Tonbridge and drove into the heavily wooded countryside beyond.

'Nearly there,' Paul observed. He looked tired but happy—a man who had nearly died, but was now returning to the beloved home of his youth. James had inherited Faversham Court on the death of their father ten years ago, and his mother had married again and was living in Australia. He had talked a great deal about his family on the way down, more than he had done in all the weeks he had spent in hospital.

Linda learnt that the Court was an old Elizabethan manor house, which had belonged to the Nicholsons since it was built in 1588, that it had been modernised after the war, 'Though Anne—my sister-in-law—is always grumbling at the lack of facilities.' That it was run by a very efficient housekeeper: 'You'll like her, Linda. She's a wonderful person.' That Anne's young sister Jackie was just back from a holiday in the States, and would be living with them from now on. 'She's a brat, but maybe she's improved now that she's left school.'

The ambulance had turned off the B-road and the woods on their left were enclosed now by a high stone wall. 'This is it,' Paul said, rising on one elbow to peer out of the smoked glass window. 'The beginning of the estate.' A few minutes later they came to an imposing entrance, with heavy pillars surmounted by stone eagles. The wrought iron gates were open. The ambulance swung through. Linda peered out at the gatehouse, half expecting a keeper to appear, so surprised was she by the unexpected grandness of it all.

'I had no idea you lived in a place like this.'

Paul smiled at her bemused tone. 'Not as impressive as it used to be in my grandfather's day. James doesn't waste money on high living—he ploughs it all back into the land.'

She thought of the distance they had already travelled since he had pointed out the beginning of the estate. 'But it's an enormous place! And you still have a lodge keeper.' She had seen smoke coming from the chimneys as they had passed.

He laughed. 'James sold the gatehouse years ago. And quite a few of the cottages which are no longer needed.' He looked at her quizzically. 'So take that uncertain expression off your face. Faversham Court's not as grand as you seem to think.'

They rounded the last bend in the drive, the woods gave way to grassland and at the bottom of a gentle slope stood the old manor house. Creeper-clad rose-red brick, mullioned windows, tall chimneys, stables and a dovecote to one side, well kept lawns, magnificent old trees. It could only seem an ordinary sort of place, 'not as grand as you think,' as Paul had just said, to someone brought up in such surroundings. To Linda, whose home wasn't as large as the outbuildings, it looked very impressive indeed.

The ambulance men were opening the back doors and preparing to lift the stretcher out.

'No!' Paul pulled himself up and waved at the wheelchair. 'You're not carrying me into the house! Lift me into that—come on, before my family arrive.'

The ambulance men looked questioningly at Linda. She nodded. 'But please be very careful of his left leg. There's not much union yet.'

They were lowering the wheelchair gently down the ramp when the front door opened and Paul's family appeared. Anne Nicholson crossed the sweep of gravel quickly, her cheeks slightly flushed, her face more animated than Linda had seen it in the past. Bending, she kissed her brother-in-law lightly on the cheek.

'Dear Paul, how glad we are to see you here!'

Straightening, she gave way to her husband. James, wearing an old tweed jacket and tough corduroys, gripped his brother hard by one shoulder. 'Anne's right, Paul. This is quite an occasion.'

A young girl came running from the house, long dark hair streaming behind her. 'Paul! Paul! I didn't hear you arrive.' She clutched him extravagantly, half laughing, half crying. She had a thin lively face, a slight unformed figure, clad in jeans and a red sweater. James introduced her as Anne's sister Jackie, but the girl hardly glanced at Linda, so taken up was she with Paul.

'Be careful,' she urged as one of the ambulance men began to push the wheelchair towards the house. 'Mind that flagstone—it's not quite level.'

'Don't fuss, Jackie,' Paul said goodhumouredly. 'They know more about it than you do.'

He was looking about him with evident pleasure. Linda and the Nicholsons followed behind, James asking courteously if they had had a good journey. The hall was spacious, stone-flagged, hung about with old family portraits. The ambulance men came to a halt, and Anne hurried up to them.

'In there.' She pointed to a door at the rear of the hall. 'We've converted the small sitting-room for you,

Paul. We thought it would be more convenient if you were on the ground floor.'

Linda was amused by the size of the small sitting-room, which was larger than the main living-room in her parents' house. However, it was bright and pleas-antly warm, with the afternoon sun streaming in through tall windows and a log fire crackling in the hearth. A wide divan bed had been placed in one corner, so that Paul could look out on to the rolling Sussex countryside.

'What a beautiful view!' Linda exclaimed, gazing at the lake and the woods beyond, golden and copper and every shade of red.

'Better than the one from my hospital room,' agreed Paul.

She turned quickly because she had caught a note of fatigue in his voice. He was smiling, but he looked very drawn, and he was rubbing the arm that had just come out of plaster.

'I think you should get into bed,' she suggested. 'You're bound to feel tired after that journey.'

He scowled like a small boy. Jackie, who was hovering impatiently in the background, gave Linda a disgusted look. 'We were going to celebrate. James has a bottle of champagne waiting in the fridge. Can't we go into the drawing-room? Take him next door,' she told the ambulance man, who still had a hold on the wheelchair.

'Calm down, Jackie,' ordered Anne. 'Paul does look tired. Nurse is right, he should have a rest.'

'Later,' growled Paul, but James backed up his wife and insisted that everyone leave the room, except Linda and the ambulance men.

They helped Paul into bed, said a cheerful goodbye and the door closed, leaving Linda alone with her patient in the pretty green and gold room.

He lay back against the pillows, looking completely

exhausted. 'You're right, my dear girl. I do feel flaked out. Give me half an hour and I'll be fine.'

There was a knock on the door and Anne came in. 'Have you everything you need, Nurse? Of course there's no washbasin in the room, but there's a cloakroom right next door, I'll sit with my brother-in-law while Mrs Nelson shows you your room.'

A flicker of irritation crossed Paul's face. 'I don't need anyone to sit with me, Anne. And do stop calling the girl Nurse. Her name is Linda Mannering.'

Anne's smile was perfunctory. 'Sorry, Nurse Mannering. I didn't mean to offend you.'

'Linda would be more friendly,' Paul suggested, to receive an affronted stare from his sister-in-law.

'I don't think that would be at all suitable. She is here in a professional capacity, after all.'

During this conversation Linda had moved towards the door. A stout white-haired woman was waiting in the hall, and they exchanged smiles.

'Shall I show Miss Mannering up, Mrs Nicholson?'

'Thank you, Mrs Nelson,' Anne said graciously, but Paul called after them.

'Is that you, Nellie? Come on in. It's ages since I've seen you.'

The housekeeper went into the room, while Linda waited in the hall, and Mrs Nicholson tapped impatiently on the floor with one elegantly shod foot. From the warm exchange of greetings it was evident that the housekeeper had known Paul all his life, and was extremely fond of him. Anne Nicholson, exasperated by the delay, pointed out that it was getting on for lunchtime.

'And I want it on time today, because I'm in court this afternoon. So if you'd show Nurse Mannering her room, please . . .'

Mrs Nelson, plainly offended, rejoined Linda in the

hall. 'This way, miss.' They mounted wide stairs with a beautifully carved handrail. 'Your room's at the end of the main corridor, and they've wired it up so that you'll hear Mr Paul's bell if need be. If you do have to go down in a hurry the back stairs are quickest.'

And more suitable? Linda wondered, remembering Anne's manner. It was plain that Paul's sister-in-law did not regard a nurse as her social equal.

Mrs Nelson opened a door and stood back for Linda. 'I hope you like it miss. If there's anything you want you only have to ask.'

It wasn't as large as Paul's room, but it was very attractive with its pretty blue floral wallpaper and its thick off white carpet. The furniture was old and well cared for. The windows looked on to the same view that she had seen from downstairs.

'It's lovely,' said Linda, and the housekeeper's face relaxed.

'I'm glad you like it. And don't forget, you only have to ask if you need anything at all. We're all very grateful for the way you've looked after Mr Paul.'

'Why, thank you, Mrs Nelson! But how did you know it was me?'

'Mr Nicholson told us. He said you've been absolutely wonderful, and that Mr Paul insisted on having you here, wouldn't even consider anyone else.'

'He might have had to,' Linda murmured, caught the housekeeper's look of incomprehension and hurried on. 'I'll be down in a few minutes, Mrs Nelson. I just want to freshen up.'

She ran a comb through her short brown hair, washed her hands and inspected her face critically. It was a pleasant face, pink-cheeked, with a wide mouth that curved easily into a smile. She had always been quite satisfied with it in the past, but now she wished that she looked more distinguished. Anne and her young sister

Jackie had bony well-bred faces, long slender hands that looked as if they had never done a day's work. They were the sort of women whom Paul must be accustomed to, since this rather grand house was his natural environment. They behaved as if they were members of the County set, which they probably were, for the Nicholsons were a very old family. Hadn't Paul told her that they had lived in this beautiful house for nearly four hundred years?

Sobered by these reflections and the realisation that it would be a waste of time getting too interested in her patient, Linda went back to his room. The whole family had gathered there, and James had a bottle of champagne in his hand.

'There you are, Nurse. Paul insisted that he felt all right. A quick celebration, then we'll have lunch.' He removed the cork expertly and as it popped out he filled the first glass for Paul. The second one he gave to Linda, then poured for his womenfolk. 'Here's to you, my dear boy, and to your speedy recovery.'

They all raised their glasses and looked towards the bed. Linda sipped and savoured the sharpness of the bubbly liquid.

'Thanks, James,' said Paul. 'Just what I needed. Better than any medicine!'

'I've got a cutting out of some newspaper, Paul, after you won a race.' Jackie crossed to the bedside and looked down eagerly at her relative by marriage. 'You've got a garland round your neck and someone's pouring champagne over your head!'

Paul grimaced at her youthful enthusiasm. 'It's part of the ritual—boring but inevitable.'

'You don't look bored in the picture,' the girl smiled. 'You've got your arm round a gorgeous blonde and she's kissing your cheek.'

'Probably some model girl out for publicity,' Paul said

carelessly, but Jackie shook her head.

'No, it isn't. It's the wife of one of the other racing drivers—it says so in the caption.'

Paul shrugged indifferently and Anne frowned. 'Do drop it, darling. Paul doesn't want to be reminded about the past.' She moved closer to the bed herself.

'Drink up, Nurse Mannering. Have some more,' urged James, but Linda shook her head and put a hand over the top of her glass.

'I'm not used to this high living, Mr Nicholson! I don't drink much at any time and never in the middle of the day.'

'Ah, but this is a special occasion.' The others were talking among themselves, so he leant towards Linda and asked what she really thought about Paul. 'Should he look so flushed? He wasn't like that last time I saw him in hospital.'

'It's probably the excitement of coming home. And the room is a little warm.'

He opened a window and the cool October air blew in. 'That's better. Do you think we should leave him now?'

'Yes, I do, Mr Nicholson.'

When James attempted to remove his womenfolk they were reluctant to go. 'Nurse Mannering thinks Paul needs a rest,' he insisted.

'He can rest all day,' Jackie pouted.

Anne said coolly, 'I think it's up to Paul to decide when he's had enough of us.'

This exchange made Linda all too conscious that her task was not going to be an easy one. Physically she would have far less to do than on the wards, less even than specialling Paul on the private wing, since he was so much better. The problems would arise because of interfering relatives. They would be in and out of his room at any time. It would be difficult to maintain a routine. It would require all her tact not to offend the Nicholson women, and a good deal of patience not to take offence herself.

It appeared that she was expected to lunch with the family, an honour which she would willingly have done without. Anne was gracious and slightly patronising, Jackie talked across her, and only James did his kindly best to make her feel at home.

When she returned to Paul's room he asked her how she was getting on. 'Think you'll like it here?'

It could do no good worrying her patient, so Linda said yes, it was a lovely place and she was going to enjoy it very much. Perhaps she overdid the enthusiasm, for he gave her a sceptical look. 'And are my relatives lovely too?'

She bit her lip and felt her colour rise. 'I'm sure we'll get on fine when I know them better. Your brother's very nice.' She saw the implications of this last sentence too late.

Paul gave one of the sarcastic smiles that she didn't like. 'Don't let Anne throw you, little one. She can be very snobbish and insensitive—doesn't even realise half the time how she puts people's backs up.'

'She's very fond of you.'

He shrugged. 'Thank God she's in court this afternoon. She takes her duties as a magistrate very seriously.'

Linda could think of no one she would less like to appear before if she were an offender than the cold and unsympathetic Anne Nicholson.

'So be a good girl and repel all invaders,' Paul went on, 'especially young Jackie. You can handle her if you have to, I hope?'

'Yes, of course.' She could be firm with a teenage girl, and James was on her side.

'Good. I feel like a nap. Why don't you explore the

grounds later? You don't have to hang around me all the time. Nellie will come if I want anything.'

So when she had settled him and made sure that no one would disturb him, Linda pulled on her duffle coat and went out for a tramp, circling the lake and entering the woods beyond. She had turned into a grassy ride that sloped gently upwards when she heard a horse's hooves behind her, and turning, she saw Jackie cantering towards her.

The girl drew up beside her and looked down with a very fair imitation of her sister's imperious manner. 'Aren't you neglecting your patient, Nurse?'

Linda assumed she was joking, but she wasn't quite sure, so she answered carefully that he was more likely to sleep if he was on his own.

'And if he wants something? He didn't look exactly well before lunch.'

Linda tried very hard to keep the irritation out of her voice. 'Mrs Nelson will listen for his bell. And it was his idea I should come out, you know.' She would have liked to tell Jackie to mind her own business and leave herself to mind the patient.

Jackie must have sensed her irritation. She flipped her hair, now in a ponytail, back over her shoulder. 'Keep your cool, Nurse Mannering. I only asked. I'm very . . . fond of Paul, you see.' She had bright blue eyes that contrasted vividly with her dark hair. She would never be pretty, but she would be a striking woman in a few years' time, like her sister Anne. 'Very fond,' she repeated, tapped her horse lightly with her whip and rode away. As she went she called over her shoulder, 'There's a superb view from the top of this ride. But don't get lost going back!'

Perhaps this was an attempt to make amends. She seemed a highly strung, intense girl, who swung disconcertingly between aggression and friendliness. In short,

Linda supposed, she was a typical teenager. And why had she put such emphasis on the words about Paul? Did she have a juvenile crush on him? Young girls often fell for older men. Paul was twenty-eight, perhaps ten or more years older than Jackie, good-looking, famous, just the sort of man to inspire teenage fantasies.

Linda thrust her hands into her coat pockets and trudged on. The view from the top was indeed superb, the English countryside at its best. She lingered longer than she had intended to, admiring the russet-coloured woods under the clear blue sky, was surprised when she found that it was nearly three-thirty, and decided she had better take a short cut back to the house.

What had looked like a short cut, however, turned out to be a blind alley with an impenetrable quickthorn hedge barring her way. Trying to find the place where she had left the path, she took a wrong turning, became hopelessly lost and spent a frustrating half hour finding her way back. It was gone four before she reached the house, flushed, breathless, hair ruffled and shoes extremely muddy. She was trying to remove the worst of the mud on the scraper by the front door when Anne appeared, accompanied by a young man.

'So there you are, Nurse,' she said coolly. 'It's a pity you weren't here for Dr Bedford's visit.'

'Doctor . . .?' Dismayed, Linda straightened and stared at the man. He had a cheerful, fresh-complexioned face and a friendly smile. If Anne was annoyed he seemed anxious to put her at ease.

'It's all right, Nurse,' he said pleasantly. 'You weren't expecting me till tomorrow, were you? But I had a call in the neighbourhood, so I thought I'd look in—more of a social visit than anything. Paul and I are old friends.'

'Yes. But I should have been here. I didn't mean to stay out so long, Mrs Nicholson. I got lost in the woods.'

'Easily done,' Dr Bedford commented. He gave Anne his wide smile. 'I'll be in tomorrow morning to see Paul professionally. Goodbye for now.'

Anne nodded and went back into the house. The young doctor turned to Linda again. 'She didn't introduce us properly. I'm Tom Bedford.'

'Linda Mannering.'

'And I understand you're from my old training school. They still turn out the prettiest nurses in London!'

He was friendly and pleasant, and Linda took to him immediately. She walked to his car, which was parked near the stables, listening carefully to what he had to say about Paul.

'Old Bonnington rang yesterday to put us in the picture.' The 'us', Linda assumed, referred to the group practice to which Tom belonged. She wondered if he would be looking after his friend medically, and when she asked this Tom shrugged.

'Why not? He prefers me. A surgeon might not want to operate on someone he knew well, but general practice is different. Anyway, Bonny says he's to have daily physiotherapy starting tomorrow, and an X-ray in a fortnight—I'll fix that with our local hospital. If there are any problems at all Bonny will come down.'

Linda watched Tom Bedford drive away, then went into the house, changed her shoes, ran a comb through her hair and went down to see her patient. He was having tea with Anne and Jackie, and was sitting in the comfortable wing chair by the fire.

'Don't you think you should have stayed in bed, Mr Nicholson?'

'No, my dear girl, and don't you start fussing! Anne said the same thing.'

'Only because I wasn't happy about helping you up,

not being a trained nurse.' A brief disapproving look at Linda. 'I feel you should take your off-duty at a more convenient time, Nurse Mannering.'

Linda felt very uncomfortable. 'It wasn't exactly off-duty. Paul—Mr Nicholson—suggested I had a breath of air, and I already told you, I got lost.'

Anne's rather thin lips had tightened at her slip. She stared at the younger woman in silence. Just so might she intimidate some offender from the bench. Linda met her eyes steadily, though she could feel her colour rising. 'Oh well!' Anne said suddenly, and gave an impatient shrug. 'I suppose no harm was done, though it might have been. More tea, Paul?'

'Thanks. Is there a cup for Linda?'

'No. If you want tea, Nurse Mannering, Mrs Nelson will give you some.'

Dismissed, Linda went quickly from the room, glad to be out of the unfriendly atmosphere, wondering if she was going to be able to stick it at Faversham Court. Tom Bedford was nice, she thought, a possible ally against Anne. And Mrs Nelson seemed all right. So she would have to learn how to cope with Anne and try hard not to give any cause for criticism. Today, she was honest enough to admit, Paul's sister-in-law had had some excuse for her displeasure. She should not have stayed out so long.

Dr Bedford arrived at eleven-fifteen next morning, accompanied by the physiotherapist, a jolly, bossy girl called Biddy Grey. After examining his patient and pronouncing himself satisfied, he left Paul to Biddy's administrations.

'She's had a call from Q.C.H. physio, so she knows what to do.' They walked together across the wide hall. 'You can give me a cup of coffee,' said Tom, pushing open the door on to the back passage and yelling for Nellie.

He was obviously quite at home in this house. Mrs Nelson looked out of the kitchen, beaming when she saw who it was. 'Dr Tom! You'll be wanting a hot drink before you're on your way. There's a fire in the library, I'll bring it in there.'

Tom threw himself into a deep leather armchair, shut his eyes and emitted a long yawn. 'Excuse me, but I was up most of the night—an awkward delivery. Had to rush her into hospital in the end.'

He revived on Nellie's steaming hot coffee, into which he spooned a copious amount of sugar. 'You'll be fat before you're forty,' Linda joked, feeling pleasantly at ease with the cheerful young doctor.

He drank three cups, pushed back his jacket sleeve, made a horrified face when he saw the time, and bounded to his feet.

'I've another five visits to make. Your fault, my dear girl, for delaying me.' He gave her a friendly thump on the shoulder. 'May I call you Linda? Walk to the car with me.'

They stood for a moment in front of the house while he fished in his pocket for the car keys. 'Coping all right?' he asked, and Linda nodded. 'Done any private nursing before?' She shook her head. 'It takes a bit of getting used to, I'm afraid. I prefer N.H.S. patients myself.'

'Oh, so do I!' exclaimed Linda with such feeling that he looked amused.

'Like that, is it? The female members of the family getting you down? Don't let them, my dear. They improve on acquaintance.'

It was easy for Tom to talk, thought Linda, as she walked back into the house. He was a school friend of Paul's. He visited the Nicholsons socially, as well as in a professional capacity. She carried the coffee tray into the kitchen and hung around, gossiping with Mrs

Nelson, not wanting to interrupt Biddy Grey's physiotherapy session.

The girl came out of Paul's room a few minutes later. 'That went very well,' she pronounced. 'He has plenty of courage—too much perhaps. Refuses to admit when he's had enough.'

Mrs Nelson insisted on serving another pot of coffee in the library. The girls exchanged information about their backgrounds, talked medical shop and found that they liked each other.

'Perhaps we could meet some time,' Biddy suggested. 'You'll be rather at a loose end in the evenings, I imagine, not knowing anyone in the district.'

In her well cut white tunic and trousers she looked smart and efficient, a sturdy compact girl with a round face and an attractive grin. 'I envy you, nursing such a dishy patient! How come they picked you?'

Linda smiled a shade ruefully. 'I fear because I'm considered sensible and down to earth. Not the sort who develops crushes on dishy men patients! Or whom patients develop crushes on either.'

What on earth had made her say that? She blushed, then went even redder when Biddy laughed uproarious. 'I wouldn't be too sure about that. He's got a very soft spot for you—sang your praises till I got positively bored!'

Biddy had a clear, carrying voice, and Anne Nicholson, who had just come into the house, stopped on her way across the hall to glance into the library. Her eyes went to the coffee cups and the plate of iced biscuits Mrs Nelson had provided. She flashed her perfunctory smile at Biddy.

'Good morning, Miss Grey. You've already treated my brother-in-law, I suppose? Are you pleased with him?'

'Yes, I am. And now I'm recovering my strength on

Mrs Nelson's excellent coffee.' Biddy took a couple of biscuits and crammed them into her mouth. 'I'm always hungry,' she confessed. 'Physio girls work darn hard.'

'Of course, my dear,' Anne agreed graciously. 'When you're finished, Nurse Mannering, I'd like a word with you.'

Linda rose quickly. 'I'm finished now, Mrs Nicholson. Biddy was just going.'

'In five minutes, then.' Anne moved to the door, the perfectly dressed countrywoman, wearing fine heather-coloured tweeds that must have cost a fortune.

'I wonder what she wants,' Linda muttered uneasily.

Biddy gave a cheerful shrug. 'Don't let her get you down. She's absolutely awful, but it's best to stand up to her. I had her as a patient last year when she fell off a horse!' She laughed and gathered up her gear. 'See you tomorrow. 'Bye for now.'

When Anne came downstairs again she had changed into grey slacks and a heavy white sweater. The only touch of colour about her was a bright lipstick. She shut the library door and came straight to the point.

'I thought it was time we had a little talk, Nurse, straightened a few things out.' There seemed nothing to say to that, so Linda remained silent. The older woman was a head taller. She looked haughtily down her long nose, a trick she had of which she might not even be aware. Linda found it decidedly offputting. She shifted uneasily and dug her nails into her palms.

Anne was good at silences. She let a few more seconds tick by before continuing. 'I understand that this is your first private case, so perhaps we should excuse your . . .' The thin mouth pursed while Anne sought for the right word. 'Your lack of savoir-faire, shall we say?'

Linda knew she was being got at, but wasn't sure what it was all about. 'I'm sorry, Mrs Nicholson,' she said slowly. (Remember what Biddy had said. She must not let Anne get her down.) 'Have I done something wrong?'

'Not exactly wrong, my dear.' Anne gave a faint, patronising smile. 'But staying in a private house has perhaps made you feel that you can waive hospital discipline, lower your standards a little, work less hard.'

Was she still going on about Linda's late return from her walk? 'I'm sorry, but could you please be more specific. What have I done that you don't like?'

'Nothing in particular, Nurse. But I sense a different attitude from the one you had in hospital, a different approach to your work.'

Linda took a deep steadying breath. 'Well, of course, Mrs Nicholson. After all, home nursing *is* different. And Mr Nicholson is no longer acutely ill. He might get fed up if I hung around him all the time. But I assure you I'm not neglecting him. I changed his dressings at nine o'clock—I have to do them twice a day.'

Her voice rose slightly with indignation, and Anne gave a brittle laugh. 'Now I've offended you. I didn't think you'd mind a little plain speaking.'

'I don't mind,' Linda answered steadily, 'and I hope you won't either. I didn't choose to be a private nurse, I was pushed into it by Sir Charles and our Principal Nursing Officer. If you're not satisfied with my work you only have to tell them.'

And that had required quite a lot of courage to get out!

Anne flushed an unbecoming red. 'You really are a touchy little thing,' she said in a high querulous voice. 'Of course no one wants you to leave. Paul would find it such a bore getting used to another girl. Just remember that you are here in a professional capacity,' and on this remark she swept out of the room.

# CHAPTER FIVE

AFTER the first few days at Faversham Court Linda began to settle into a proper routine with her patient. Breakfast at seven, because she knew he slept badly and was always awake very early. Then the tedious and time consuming business of attending to his dressings, getting him ready for Biddy's visits and on some days for Tom Bedford as well. Those days he didn't pay an official visit, Tom usually looked in for a chat, often at teatime, occasionally in the evening.

Linda's early apprehension about life with the Nicholsons had not been entirely dispelled. What Anne had called 'plain speaking' had seemed for a few days to clear the air. If her manner wasn't exactly warm at least it was no longer hypercritical, but Linda sensed that she was not liked either by Anne or her young sister. There was nothing positive on which she could put her finger, just a general sense of constraint, of being constantly reminded that they regarded her as an inferior.

She had a sufficient sense of her own worth and sufficient pride in her work not to let this attitude depress her. She thought Anne and Jackie two of the most snobbish people she had ever met, and wondered why the men of the family should be so much nicer. Paul had faults, but he was not a snob. As for James, although he was out a great deal on estate business, when she did meet him he was unfailingly courteous and friendly.

So on the whole she found life fairly agreeable, and even began to enjoy living in the beautiful old house with its magnificent gardens. After the unfortunate incident on the first day, she was always careful about her off-duty, only going out when she was officially free. She spent a great deal of time with Paul, pushing him around the grounds in his wheelchair when the weather was fine, chatting and reading to him, because he still suffered from frequent headaches as a result of concussion at the time of the accident.

She no longer worried about becoming emotionally involved with him, and even considered herself rather silly for ever imagining that she might. She acknowledged his attraction without letting it affect her, accepted the fact that he could take his pick of available women, so was scarcely likely to encourage her, an ordinary unglamorous working girl from a very different background from his own.

If she was absolutely honest with herself, it had cost her a pang or two and several restless nights to reach this sensible conclusion, but as a result she felt more at ease in his company. Most of the time, anyhow. Now and then he could still say things that upset her.

One day when she brought in his tea-tray, he gestured at the three cups on it. 'Tom coming?'

'Perhaps,' she said. It had become a habit that she and Paul had breakfast and tea together. She suspected that Anne didn't really approve, but it was Paul who insisted.

He was smiling now, watching her as she poured. 'I wonder if Tom would have come so often if it had been someone else.'

'Someone else?'

'Some other nurse. The sexy blonde, for instance.'

It took her a few moments to grasp his meaning, then she blushed deeply. 'He comes to see you. He's a good friend.'

'Oh, sure,' Paul said easily, 'but I don't flatter myself that I'm the main attraction. No, I don't think the sexy blonde would have been his type.'

'Do stop using that silly expression! Her name's Marianne Littlewood and she's quite a nice girl.'

'Only quite nice?' he laughed. 'You look beautiful when you blush. Has Tom asked you out yet?'

The blush deepened. She nearly told him that it was none of his business, changed her mind and admitted that Tom had. 'He's taking me out to dinner on Saturday evening.'

'Good.' He looked approving. 'For a young girl you don't have much fun, stuck down here in the country.'

'I don't mind,' Linda said earnestly. 'I was brought up in the country. I prefer it really.'

Paul toyed with a piece of bread and butter, still suffering from the lack of appetite that worried her. 'Do you?' he asked with a heavy sigh. 'I can't say that I do.'

'You're difficult to please, Paul. You sneer at the showbiz side of motor racing—you called it brash and vulgar only the other day—and now you're implying you miss it.'

'Not the racing as such, or the endless travelling. I suppose what I really miss is city life. I'm not a true countryman at heart like James. Just as well, isn't it, that he's the elder son?'

He looked so fed up that she felt the need to cheer him. 'I'm sure you'll be able to move back to your London flat before long. You'd need someone to run it for you, though, and you'd have to go on with your physio for quite a long time.'

He brightened at this idea and was silent for a minute or two, then he spoke again. 'I suppose I could go any time if I organised things properly. How about moving in with me as resident nurse-cum-housekeeper?'

Linda thought at first that he was joking, but when she made a casual reply he told her that he was perfectly serious. 'Well, Linda? How about it? You don't like it

here that much. I can tell that you find my sister-in-law
a pain in the neck. And dear Jackie's almost as bad.'

'I'm used to them now. And you must know it's impossible.'

'Why?'

'Well . . .' She stared at him rather helplessly, unable
to formulate her thoughts, very conscious of his steady
gaze and the beginning of a smile. He still had the ability
to confuse her on occasion, knew it and was amused by
it, darn him, she thought resentfully.

'Linda dear,' he said gently, 'you're surely not being
stuffy and conventional? Not worrying about what
people would say?' She bit her lip and he started to
laugh. 'What a funny girl you are! I *am* still an invalid.
Even the gossip columnists could scarcely imagine an
affair between us, with me as I am now.' He gestured
disparagingly at his plastered leg and she smiled faintly
in return.

'I know, Paul, but——' She knew that his idea would
be unwise, for her if not for him. There were still times
when she found him too attractive, though she couldn't
offer that as a reason. 'Your brother and his wife would
be very put out,' she began again, relieved to have
something positive to say. 'It would hurt their feelings,
Paul. You know that.'

'I doubt it,' he said, oddly abrupt. 'James might be
relieved to see me go.' He rested his head against the
back of the chair, looking tired and extremely strained.

Her eyes widened in surprise. She was about to ask
him what on earth he meant when Tom opened the
door, and the opportunity was lost. She went off to the
kitchen for a fresh pot of tea, still puzzling over Paul's
remark. The brothers seemed so fond of each other, and
yet occasionally there was a hint of strain between them.
And Paul had most definitely been reluctant to come
down here in the first place. She remembered how Sir

Charles had had to persuade him.

When she came back the two men were discussing ways of relieving Paul's boredom. 'He's being more patient than I expected,' Tom remarked to Linda, 'and now I think it's time we let him off the hook a bit. Sir Charles rang this morning to say that his latest X-rays show good progress. I suggest you take him out for short drives while the good weather lasts. He needs a change of surroundings to cheer him up.' Tom glanced from Paul to Linda, pleased at his solution to the problem.

'Take him out? Me? You mean I'd have to drive?' She looked so horrified that the two men laughed.

'Why not?' asked Paul.

'I should feel shy, driving you.' The ready colour sprang into her cheeks. 'Couldn't one of the family take you?'

'James is too busy.'

'Mrs Nicholson?'

'Not Anne,' he said dismissively.

'Then Jackie? I'm sure she'd be delighted.'

'Jackie's just passed her test at the third attempt.' He pulled a face. 'I'd feel safer with you.'

'We-ell . . .' Still she hesitated. 'I know Mrs Nicholson is pretty busy, but I'm sure she wouldn't mind.'

Paul started to frown, and Tom, after a quick look at his friend's face, urged Linda to agree. 'He won't eat you if you crash the gears, and it'll be a pleasant change for you as well.'

She walked out to the car with him, as she often did. 'I suppose it is a good idea, taking Paul out,' she remarked. 'At least I shall feel I'm earning my keep. Mrs Nicholson drops the odd snide remark about the cushy time I'm having.'

'And that bothers you?'

'Of course it does, because I half agree with her. There

are such hours when I do absolutely nothing.'

'Except keeping the patient as happy as possible. Which you ought to know is a very important part of therapy,' Tom said firmly. 'Don't let Anne's stupid ideas get you down.'

She sighed and Tom put a brotherly arm around her shoulders. On a sudden impulse she told him of Paul's desire to return to London.

He looked surprised, then he shook his head. 'Absolutely not on, my dear. Why do you think Bonny agreed to him coming down here, when he wasn't really ready for it?' She shook her head and he told her that Sir Charles had decided the quiet of the country would be beneficial to his patient. 'He disapproved of all those visitors—said they were wearing Paul out. He asked Anne to put people off coming here, except for a few close friends.' He grinned suddenly. 'What did you think of Paul's girls?'

Linda didn't want to sound priggish and uncharitable, so she hesitated before speaking. 'I didn't really have much to do with them.'

His smile widened. 'I can tell you didn't think much of them.'

'Well . . . they seemed so artificial . . . frothy . . . you know! I'm amazed that Paul could want to spend time with women like that.'

'Are you, Linda? But you don't know Paul that well, do you?'

'I've nursed him for nearly two months. You learn a lot about someone when you're with them all day.'

'Perhaps.' He felt for his car keys. 'But the Paul you're seeing is a very different man from the Grand Prix driver. When he's back in that world—if he goes back to it—you'd hardly recognise him.'

He got into his car and drove off, leaving Linda staring after him, and thinking with a vague sense of depression about what he had just said. She liked Paul. She wanted to think well of him. She was reluctant to believe that he belonged with those silly, frivolous girls. Sighing, she walked back into the house and busied herself with preparing the dressing tray, for some of Paul's wounds were still not completely healed.

Next day at lunch Anne was plainly in a bad mood, and not for the first time Linda wished she could have eaten with Paul or Mrs Nelson. However, she was expected to eat with the family, which today consisted only of the two Nicholsons. Anne criticised the fish, which Linda thought delicious, grumbled because the gardener hadn't swept the leaves off the big lawn, and was generally extremely disagreeable.

At the end of the meal, when Linda asked to be excused, she said in her most acid tones,' Please wait, Nurse. I have something to say to you.'

'Something to say' from Anne meant trouble. Linda subsided again on to her chair and waited to hear what she had done wrong.

Anne studied her well manicured nails for a few moments. 'Was it your idea to take my brother-in-law out for drives?'

Linda looked up quickly. 'No, Mrs Nicholson, it was Tom's—Dr Bedford's,' she added quickly, knowing how Anne disapproved when she used christian names.

Anne's lips thinned. She turned to James, who was finishing his coffee. 'It's a ridiculous idea. Most unsuitable, don't you agree, darling?'

James grunted noncommittally, as he often did when appealed to by his wife. Anne looked irritated and swung back to Linda.

'So I suggest you forget about it, Nurse Mannering.'

'But . . . I thought it was all fixed. He's looking forward to a trip this afternoon. I think he'll be quite disappointed if we don't go.'

Anne gave her a haughty stare. 'Then I shall drive him.'

Linda remembered Paul's reaction when she had suggested just that. 'Not Anne,' he had said tersely. Well, there was nothing she could do about it. 'Is that all, Mrs Nicholson?' she asked politely.

Anne, having got her own way, became almost gracious. 'Thank you, Nurse. Tell my brother-in-law I'll be ready in ten minutes.'

As Linda left the room she caught the other woman's remark, 'I don't want that girl getting ideas about Paul,' and James' quick, 'Hush, Anne!' his voice much sharper than usual.

When Linda told her patient that Anne would be taking him out he reacted with surprising vehemence. 'Absolute rubbish! We agreed that you should. Why didn't you tell her?'

'I did try to, but Mrs Nicholson can be . . .' She hesitated and smiled at him rather uncertainly.

Paul didn't return her smile. 'Go away, my dear girl. Leave me to deal with Anne.'

'I don't think——'

'Off you go, Linda. Come back in half an hour.'

When she returned he was on his own, in his usual chair by the fire, his crutches in front of him. 'Ready? Let's go, then.'

She didn't ask, and he didn't tell her, what Anne's reaction had been. James, looking harassed, helped her to get his brother into the estate car, which was judged to be the most convenient for a disabled man. They lowered the back seat, put a mattress in and a pile of cushions, so that Paul could stretch out comfortably with his plastered leg adequately supported.

The fine autumn weather continued and their afternoon outings became a regular occurrence, except for the occasional day when Paul didn't feel up to it. Anne made no secret of her disapproval, dropping acid remarks about Linda's inexperience as a driver, and about the setback to Paul if he should have another accident.

'Oh, come on, darling,' James objected, as they were leaving the lunch table one day. 'I'm sure Linda is extremely careful.' He gave his slow attractive smile that was a little like Paul's, and Linda smiled back at him.

'I am very careful. Honestly, Mrs Nicholson, you don't have to worry about me.'

'It's Paul she's worrying about, not you, Nurse,' Jackie interposed rudely.

James frowned at his young sister-in-law. 'That was quite uncalled for, Jackie!'

Jackie shrugged and tossed her dark hair back, and Linda, embarrassed by the disagreeable behaviour of the other two women, left the room quickly.

It was a relief to get out of the house and she had already lost her selfconsciousness about driving Paul. In spite of Anne's fears she was perfectly competent, even if she had not done a great deal of driving. Paul would pick a fresh route each afternoon, so that already they had covered miles of the lush Sussex countryside.

'Turn left at the bottom of the drive,' he ordered as they set out, 'then left again at the crossroads.'

After a few minutes Linda forgot about the unpleasant little incident at lunch and began to enjoy herself. Everything was so beautiful, the autumn colours vivid in the sunshine. At the top of a hill Paul suggested that she park on a stretch of grass and look at the view.

'It's the highest point for miles. I used to come here for picnics as a boy.'

She had left her seat and come round to the back of the car. She opened the doors and he inhaled deeply, stretching his arms out as he did so. He smiled up at her and she caught her breath, because he was so attractive. Act normally, she thought, don't let him realise how he affects you.

Paul patted the mattress on which he lay. 'Sit down. You can see quite well from here.'

After a few moments' hesitation she sat on the extreme edge of the mattress and stared down the hill. Paul asked suddenly, 'Do you have to wear that uniform?'

She looked at him in surprise. 'Of course I do. I am still a nurse.'

'I should have thought that off duty——'

'But I'm not off duty,' she said quickly, very conscious of his closeness. With some idea of stressing her medical role, though why she should need to she wasn't quite clear, she added another remark. 'Tom says keeping you happy is an important part of therapy.'

'Does he indeed?' He leant forward and took her hand in his. 'How do you think he meant you to do that?' he asked softly. She tried to move away, but he held on to her hand. He was smiling now, as if he knew only too well the effect he had on her. 'Well, Linda? What do you think he meant you to do?'

'I—I don't know,' she stammered. 'I mean—n-nothing special. He was just generalising . . .'

Her words tailed away as Paul leant closer and put an arm round her shoulders. 'This is the best form of therapy I know,' he smiled, and kissed her on the mouth.

Outraged, she shoved him away, so that he fell back against the cushions and she was worried for a moment, in case she might have hurt him. However, he continued to smile, so she said crossly, 'I'm not one of your girls, Paul! You know quite well Tom didn't mean that.'

He lay back looking very amused. 'I don't suppose he did. Bit of an old spoilsport, is Tom. Besides, he fancies you himself!'

She rose with dignity and backed away from the car. 'If you're bored with life, Mr Nicholson, you'd better invite one of your girl-friends down. They wouldn't mind being kissed, I'm sure!'

'Prissy little thing, aren't you?' he remarked carelessly. 'What's a kiss between friends?'

'I'm not your friend, Mr Nicholson. I'm your nurse, and I'd rather you kept that in mind.' She shut her door with a bang and switched on the ignition. As they moved away she looked in the driving mirror and saw that Paul was watching her, caught his eye and laughed in spite of herself. It was impossible to be annoyed with him for long, but she wasn't going to let him kiss her, just because she was the only woman available!

The afternoon trips continued, but Paul was careful not to offend her again. Sometimes she felt that he overdid the formality, and suspected him of mocking her. However, it was better than excessive familiarity, so it was silly of her to mind.

There was so much about him that still puzzled her. One afternoon, when they were passing through a particularly pretty village, he commented on the new bungalows on the outskirts.

'There've been a lot of changes since I was last here.'

'Those bungalows have been here for years,' observed Linda, looking at their well established gardens. 'Perhaps you just didn't notice them.'

'I haven't been this way for five years.'

The village was quite close to Faversham and on a main road. 'Really?' she said, faintly surprised. 'I should have thought you were bound to go through it some time.'

'I live in London when I'm in England.' He indicated a wide area by the village green suitable for parking.

'But you used to visit your brother, surely?' Linda

asked, switching off the engine.

An odd expression crossed his face. 'I haven't stayed at Faversham for years.' At her astonished look he added quietly, 'We used to meet occasionally in London.'

'But why——' Discretion made her halt, for it was none of her business. To cover any awkwardness she got out of the car and walked over to the old well. As she stood by it, pretending to study it, she puzzled over Paul's relations with his family. The one certain thing seemed to be that the brothers must have had a serious disagreement, and yet they *were* fond of each other. James had been very upset by Paul's accident. Linda supposed their occasional meetings in London had been an attempt to conceal the rift from other people.

When she returned to the car Paul still had the strained look that any reference to the past brought to his face. Feeling guilty at being the cause of it, she did her best to change the subject. 'This is such a pretty place. Do they ever play cricket on the green?'

He smiled. 'They certainly used to. I captained the Faversham team against them once when I was a boy.' The lines of strain had gone now, though they lingered on in Linda's memory.

They were later returning home than usual. When Linda drew up before the front door Jackie came running out of the house.

'There's a visitor for you, Paul. He's been waiting ages. Hugh Mansel.'

'He should have let me know he was coming,' said Paul, edging towards the car's rear doors and grasping his crutches.

'Didn't realise you were well enough to go out for drives, old chap.' Hugh Mansel, Paul's team manager, whom Linda had met in hospital, came strolling out accompanied by Anne. The two men exchanged a warm handgrip, then Hugh helped Paul into the wheelchair.

Somehow it was Anne who wheeled him into the house, with Hugh close behind. When Linda made to follow them into Paul's room Jackie caught her by the arm.

'Don't you think you've monopolised him for long enough?' Her manner was unpleasant, her expression disagreeable, but since the girl often made remarks like this Linda paid little attention.

'I'd better see if he wants anything.'

'If he does he can tell the others.' Jackie's hand was still on her arm. 'You can fetch their tea,' she said haughtily. 'That's what you're here for, isn't it?'

It was not, though Linda, like all good nurses, never minded helping out with domestic chores. She had got into the habit of preparing Paul's breakfast because he liked it at seven, and Mrs Nelson was scarcely up at that time.

'Are you trying to be nasty, Jackie?' Linda asked, keeping her voice deliberately light. 'And if so, what on earth for?'

The younger girl's face became spiteful and lost all its attractiveness. 'I'm sick of the way you monopolise Paul—all those cosy little sessions in the car. Have you got him to make love to you yet? That's what you're after, isn't it?'

Linda gasped, astounded by the venom in Jackie's voice. 'You're being quite ridiculous! Paul is my patient. I take him out because his doctor suggested it.'

'Oh yes,' sneered Jacky, 'and doubtless you leapt at the idea! You're hoping he'll fall for you, aren't you? But Paul likes trendy girls—he's too sophisticated to waste time on a nobody like you.' Her scornful glance raked Linda's slim figure in the crisp navy uniform, with its white collar and cuffs.

There was an air of suppressed violence about her that Linda found extremely disturbing. Could Jackie's emotional behaviour be the cause of Paul's estrangement from his brother? Surely not, for if he hadn't been home for five years, Anne's sister would have been a little girl when they last met.

There was one way to find out—ask! 'Do you always go on like this about the poor man?' Linda queried. 'Was it because of you that he stopped coming down?'

Her question made Jackie stare for a few moments, then she reacted angrily. 'Of course it wasn't because of me! I used to meet him in London sometimes. It was because of——' She bit off the end of the sentence and scowled at Linda. 'So you listen to gossip, Nurse Mannering. I wonder who's been blabbing about us.'

To Linda's relief Mrs Nelson appeared at that moment. Jackie, who had been about to add something else, swung away across the hall, flushed and angry. The housekeeper couldn't have heard this extraordinary conversation, but she had seen enough to know that the two girls had been having some sort of dispute.

'What's Madam up to now?' she asked sympathetically, as Linda followed her into the kitchen to fetch Paul's tea.

'Oh, she has some bee in her bonnet,' Linda answered vaguely, and on a sudden impulse she added, 'Mrs Nelson, would you mind awfully taking in the tea today?' She sat down at the kitchen table, more shaken by the incident with Jackie than she cared to admit.

Mrs Nelson, after one look at her distressed face, said that of course she would, and Linda must have tea with her today. Doubtless Mr Mansel would be stopping for some time. She bustled out of the kitchen with the tray and Linda slumped in her chair, wondering what madness had got into Jackie, and how they could meet after such unpleasantness without embarrassment.

Of course the girl was obsessively jealous, absurd though that was. Jealous and possessive, in the throes of a violent infatuation for her brother-in-law, made worse by the fact that she had too much time for brooding. She had left school in July, having failed all her A-levels, and seemed unable to decide what to do with herself.

Linda sighed and wondered how to handle the situation. Such a pity, she thought regretfully, that she hadn't just walked away from Jackie when she made that first disagreeable remark. Should she say something about it to Anne, in case Jackie complained first? No, Anne would only back up her sister, and somehow make Linda feel at fault. And it wasn't the sort of thing she could mention to James.

Tom, then? Yes, Tom was the one. Tomorrow was one of his official visiting days, so when he had said goodbye to Paul, Linda asked Mrs Nelson for coffee and took him into the library. She shut the door firmly, but found it difficult to start. Was she making too much out of a silly hysterical girl's infatuation? Hesitantly, feeling rather foolish but determined to tell him the whole story, she ploughed on.

'If it just involved me I expect I could cope,' she ended, 'but Paul gets upset if he senses any disagreement between us. Which there often is,' she added with a sigh. She looked uncertainly at Tom's frowning face. 'You think I'm being silly, I expect, but it's left an unpleasant taste in my mouth. And last night at dinner—James insists that I eat with them——'

'So I should hope!'

'Yes—well—Jackie sulked and Anne kept asking her what was wrong. Thank heavens she didn't say, but I felt terribly uncomfortable.'

'Do you want me to talk to her?' Tom asked. 'I doubt it would do much good. She's just a silly little girl. Partly Paul's fault, of course, for taking her out occasionally when she was at school in London.'

'She probably invited herself,' Linda observed, and he laughed.

'More than likely. Does he realise how she feels about him, do you think?'

'I should have thought it was pretty obvious. No wonder the poor man looks so tense sometimes!' She was silent, worrying away at the problem. 'Tom, it isn't only Jackie that bothers Paul. What *is* the mystery about them all? If I understood a bit more I'd be less likely to drop bricks.'

His expression was curious. 'I don't think we should be talking like this, Linda. It has nothing to do with Paul's health, which is your only concern.'

That was as near to a snub as he could possibly get. At her hurt look he relented. 'I didn't mean to snap, dear girl, but the past is better forgotten. I'm so glad that they're friends again.' He made a determined effort to change the subject. 'Now about Paul's leg. It's to come out of plaster on Monday. It's to be X-rayed again on Monday, and if it's satisfactory he's to start weight bearing after that.'

# CHAPTER SIX

HUGH Mansel was the first of Paul's friends to visit him at Faversham, and now that his general condition was so much better, Paul insisted that it was entertainment he needed rather than rest.

'It'll let Linda off the hook a bit. She hardly has any time to herself.'

The family were gathered in the drawing-room. Paul was able to move around more easily now and insisted that he no longer needed meals in his room, or to go to bed early.

Anne smiled thinly. 'Nurse Mannering has the regulation off-duty, Paul.'

'Of course.' He rested his head against the back of the sofa and looked at Linda through half-closed eyes, a trick he had which did things to her pulse. 'However, she must be heartily sick of humouring me. Confess it, my dear. I haven't been the easiest of patients.' The smile he gave her was both intimate and charming.

It reminded her of the time that he had kissed her. She was trying to think of a light rejoinder, but Anne spoke first, after exchanging an expressive glance with her young sister. 'I'm sure Nurse Mannering has no complaints.' And Jackie added under her breath, 'Because she knows when she's on to a good thing, of course.'

Paul, who was on the other side of the fireplace, missed this remark, but Linda didn't, and the colour rushed into her cheeks. James, immersed as usual in a farming journal, was taking no part in the conversation.

Anne shook her head warningly at Jackie, then she

smiled at her brother-in-law. 'Nurse Mannering won't have to put up with you for much longer, will she? I can't see why you need a nurse at all, now you're so much better.'

Paul shrugged. 'The experts seem to think I do.'

'The district nurse could come in if you needed anything. Then Nurse Mannering could get back to her real work.'

Paul laughed. 'Don't I rate as real work? How unflattering!'

The conversation changed, but Linda continued to feel uncomfortable, for she had a strong impression that Anne wanted her to leave as soon as possible. Had Jackie told her about the other day? Or hinted perhaps in her outrageous way that Linda was making a play for Paul?

Next evening, which she was spending at Biddy Grey's place, she brought up the matter. Biddy had a nice little flat in the nearest country town. The two girls had eaten supper and were sitting on the hearthrug in front of the coal fire, when Linda told her friend about her problems.

'It's an unpleasant feeling suspecting you're not wanted. I told you about Jackie's remarks, but I didn't realise that Anne disliked me quite so much.'

Biddy looked very thoughtful. 'I wonder if there's anything in that old story. You know that Paul and Anne were friends before she married James?'

Biddy was a local girl and knew everything that went on for miles around. 'No, I didn't know,' Linda answered slowly. 'You mean ... Paul knew her first?' Could that be why Paul had stayed away from Faversham in the last few years? Because his brother had taken his girl away? 'Were they in love, do you think?' she asked, and Biddy stretched out her sturdy legs in their red tights and yawned luxuriously.

'Dunno. They could have been. He's a devastatingly attractive man, isn't he? Oh, to be beautiful, or at least elegant and well born, like horrible Anne! Could he love a woman like that?'

'Quite easily, I should think. He sees her from a different angle, after all. She doesn't talk down to him.'

The idea of this possible past love affair gave her no pleasure. And what if it was not past? What if Paul still loved his brother's wife? That could account for his reluctance to live in the same house as her. Perhaps explain the hordes of girl-friends, none of whom seemed to have captured her heart.

'I shall be glad when I finish here!' she exclaimed suddenly. 'Anne's right, I'm not really needed any more.'

Biddy poked at the fire. 'Tom will miss you. He likes you a lot.'

'And I like him. If he wants to keep in touch London's not that far away.'

'Know something?' said Biddy, still doing things to the fire. 'If you want to avoid unpleasantness with Paul's womenfolk, all you have to do is to show more interest in Tom.'

Linda stared at the back of her friend's head, not quite sure if she was serious. The other girl swung round suddenly, flushed from the fire. 'He's very keen, but you play it so cool. He can't tell where he is with you.'

'How can you possibly know that?'

'Because Tom confides in me. We've known each other a long time.'

Not over-pleased at the idea of being discussed by Tom and Biddy, however much she liked them both, Linda frowned into the fire. 'Honestly, you make it sound like a sit-com on the TV! I encourage Tom to stop Jackie and Anne being jealous. It's absolutely farcical, especially when there's nothing for them to be jealous about.'

'I'm not too sure about that,' Biddy said slowly, and at Linda's exclamation, 'You look awfully sweet in your uniform. If a girl's at all nice-looking a nurse's gear does something for her.'

Linda laughed rather ruefully. 'Jackie doesn't think so. She said I was a nobody.'

'Just being spiteful. I should say Paul would find you a refreshing change after all those boring glamour girls he racketed around with in the past.'

Perhaps he did, but he would forget her as soon as she no longer nursed him. He wouldn't want to meet her, as some of her expatients had done. Biddy was pursuing her own line of thought still.

'So you see maybe Jackie—and possibly Anne—do have grounds for being jealous. And can you honestly say that if Paul showed an interest in you you wouldn't encourage him?'

The two girls stared at one another. Linda went very pink and looked away first. 'I don't think of Paul in that way,' she said lamely.

'Liar!' Biddy retorted, but not unkindly.

It was noticeable that the glamour girls, as Biddy had called them, continued to stay away. Indeed, nearly all Paul's visitors were men, and Linda couldn't help wondering if Anne had something to do with this, or if it was Paul's own wish.

Hugh Mansel came frequently whenever he was in England, and brought his star driver first-hand news of the Grand Prix circuits. Linda gathered that the last Formula One race had occurred early in October, and that the team managers were now mainly preoccupied over who to sign up for the following season. Also that, but for his accident, even if he hadn't won the World Championship, Paul could have taken his pick of the top racing combines.

'Absolute rubbish,' Paul commented. 'You know quite well, Hugh, that nothing could have lured me away from the Medway team.'

Hugh gave a slow smile as he looked at his friend, stretched out on the sofa in front of the drawing-room fire. The rest of the family were out this afternoon, so Linda was enjoying a quiet tea with the two men.

'Anyone of half a dozen of our rivals would have snapped you up for a large sum of money, Paul.'

'I don't need the money,' Paul shrugged, 'so perhaps I'm less easy to corrupt than some people! Anyway, Hugh, that's all in the past.' He frowned down at his left leg, still encased in plaster more than two months after his accident.

Sir Charles had been to see him recently and Linda knew that the surgeon had been disappointed by his latest X-ray. Paul, who was a realist, had insisted on being told the truth, and he knew that his medical advisers were not pleased with his orthopaedic progress, though his general condition was excellent.

Hugh said quietly, 'You may not be fit for next season, but surely by the one after?'

Paul stared into the fire. 'No one knows for sure.'

'I'm sure,' Linda cut in, because she hated to see how depressed he was looking. No young and healthy man could fail to make a good recovery in eighteen months. 'You should be driving again long before that.'

'Oh, driving!' Paul exclaimed dismissively. 'Of course I'll be driving, but shall I be racing? I doubt it. If I'm not as good as I was before Zandvoort, then I don't want to be in the game at all.'

When he was leaving Hugh said he had forgotten some photographs he wanted to give Paul. Would Linda walk out to the car with him to fetch them? Faintly surprised that he didn't fetch them himself, she complied, and soon realised that it was only an excuse. Hugh had some questions to ask about his friend.

Were his medical advisers really worried about Paul? Did people with his type of leg fractures often have permanent disabilities? Linda answered as best she could. Hugh listened carefully, his face sombre.

'It will be unspeakably rotten luck if he's never as good again. Especially as it was another driver's lunacy that put him where he is.'

Paul had never told her much about the accident. When she asked what had happened Hugh said laconically, 'Oh, this young idiot who hit him has an unfortunate habit of running into other drivers! He got off scot free himself.'

She asked him if Paul had really been as good as everyone said he was. Hugh smiled faintly.

'Most drivers spend years trying to reach Formula One. Paul was a natural, celebrated in two seasons.' He handed her the photographs. 'These may cheer him up a bit. Do your best to keep him happy, Linda. He relies on you a great deal.'

Those words pleased her more than she cared to admit. 'Of course I will,' she promised earnestly. 'If he can't race again, what will he do for a living?'

Hugh smiled down at her solemn young face. 'Go back to what he was doing before he started racing.'

'And that was?'

He looked surprised. 'Has no one told you? Designing.' She gazed back at him blankly. 'Design engineering. Designing cars,' he explained.

'Paul's an engineer?' She couldn't have been more astonished.

'Yes. He took an engineering degree at Cambridge, got interested in racing and teamed up with Ronald Medway. You have heard of Medway?' he asked, gently teasing.

'Of course,' she said indignantly. 'Medways are the cars that Paul used to drive. I had absolutely no idea that he was anything more than a first-class racing driver.'

She walked back into the house, very thoughtful. These revelations cut across all her preconceived ideas of Paul, the public hero and heart-throb. She gave him the photographs, told him what Hugh had said, then asked him why he had first started racing.

He spread his hands wide. 'A designer likes to try out his designs. I found I had a flair for fast driving and I got hooked, that's all.'

'Who is more important? The designer or the driver?'

He smiled. 'To win a Grand Prix race you need a car that works and a driver who makes fewer mistakes than anyone else on the circuit.'

'So both are equally important?'

'You could say that.'

'Then if you have to—I mean if you do decide to retire—you could still be very much a part of the motor racing world, couldn't you?'

'What is this?' he asked irritably. 'Did Hugh tell you to give me a pep talk?'

Linda coloured. 'He's worried about you. He thinks you're losing heart.'

He shifted restlessly on the sofa. 'I'm getting fed up with the inactivity. How about driving me up to London, little one? There are one or two things I want to collect from my flat, a couple of people I want to see.'

Anne was often in London. 'Mrs Nicholson could fetch them for you,' Linda suggested, not liking the idea of driving through the centre of London, for she knew Paul's flat was in Hampstead.

'No, I'd prefer to go myself. If you don't fancy driving I'll find someone else.'

*

In the end it was Tom who drove Paul up to London on his day off from the surgery, which was always a Wednesday. Linda went with them, at Paul's suggestion.

'You'd like a break from Faversham, wouldn't you? There's no point your staying here when I'm elsewhere.'

It would be nice to see some of her friends, get some early Christmas shopping done, have a day out in the city, away from Anne and Jackie.

They left very early, Linda sitting beside Tom, Paul with his plastered leg stretched out on the back seat and a pile of cushions behind him. Their mood was carefree and relaxed. The two men teased Linda and made her laugh. She was happy in their company and pleased to think that she was looking her best, in a new blue outfit she had bought in Tunbridge Wells only last week.

'I like that get-up,' Tom had said, eyeing the little suede waistcoat and matching skirt, as she walked out to the car beside Paul.

Paul hadn't commented on her appearance when she gave him his breakfast, but he had looked her over with a smiling approval that had brought a blush to her cheeks. However often she told herself to ignore it, there were times when she found his physical attraction quite overpowering. Times when he made her pulse race and breath come faster. When she would long and long to be in his arms again, only this time she would not repulse him—outrageous ideas for a dedicated young nurse to have about her patient. Dreams she must not indulge in for her own peace of mind.

Tom drove fast and competently. They threaded easily through the centre of London to Chalk Farm, climbed Haverstock Hill and turned into the Hampstead side road where Paul's flat was. It was the ground floor of a converted Victorian house, spacious and bright, with a view towards the Heath.

Paul, looking extremely pleased to be in his own home again, lowered himself on to the sofa. 'Be a dear girl and make some coffee. The kitchen's at the back of the hall.'

When she returned with the tray he was on the telephone, talking technical racing jargon to some member of his team. Linda looked around the large living-room, which gave on to an attractive paved area that seemed to be walled off from the rest of the garden.

'Yes, that part's mine,' Paul told her. 'The main garden goes with the first floor flat.'

The patio had climbing plants on the wall, evergreens in tubs, a small pool in the centre. 'It's very attractive,' Linda said, and Tom grinned.

'Even more so when Paul's girl-friends are adorning it! Do you remember that party when Lisa Cantelli came? And Fenella Freeman? Wow!' Tom was a simple soul and impressed by famous names.

Paul said nothing. He stirred his coffee, drank and helped himself to a biscuit.

'The air was absolutely electric!' Tom went on, turning to Linda. 'Everyone could see that those two girls hated each other's guts.' He heaved a dramatic overdone sigh. 'What I'd give to be a heart-throb like this chap!'

'Oh, for God's sake, Tom, belt up. Linda doesn't want to hear you drivelling on.'

Offended, Tom relapsed into silence, and Linda was left to her own thoughts. Unhappy ones, because she was forced to acknowledge what she had always known, yet been reluctant to admit. Paul belonged in a different world. Such contact as she had with him was strictly temporary, a consequence of his accident and her professional skills. If by some chance they had met in the ordinary way, he would not have looked twice at her. Depressed, she finished her coffee and rose.

'I'll be off now. What time shall we meet?'

Tom, who seemed to have recovered his usual ebulli-
ence, suggested around six. 'You'll probably be tired by
then, Paul. You're not quite as well as you think you
are.' He turned to Linda. 'Twelve o'clock, then, outside
the Underground.' He had asked her to have lunch with
him and Linda had accepted.

Now she hesitated, looking a little anxiously at her
patient. 'Are you sure you'll be all right on your own?
How soon is your friend coming?'

Paul looked at his watch. 'In less than an hour. No
need to worry about me—I shan't move from this sofa.
Leave the catch up and he can let himself in.'

'But your lunch——'

'There's an excellent take away place just around the
corner. I often use it. Johnny can pick up something
when we're hungry. Now off you go and enjoy yourselves.' He smiled at them both and was reaching for
the telephone again before they were through the door.

'He hates being fussed over,' Tom remarked as he
held the car door for Linda. 'But I agree that he
shouldn't be alone for too long. If he had an accident
and fell, it wouldn't do that leg of his any good.'

He was dropping her off near Oxford Street and they
were meeting again near Q.C.H. Linda shopped all
morning, had an enjoyable lunch with Tom and then
met a couple of her friends who were off duty in the
afternoon.

Angie wanted to hear all about her exploits in what
she insisted on calling the stockbroker belt. 'Have you
met lots of lovely rich men, with super cars and dis-
honourable intentions?' Angie always made a joke of
things. She bubbled with vitality and joie-de-vivre, so
that it was impossible to remain depressed in her company.

Smiling, Linda said that such rich men as she had

met at the Nicholsons' house were middle-aged and married. 'Farming types mainly, I think. They go in for hunting and point-to-pointing. And their wives wear gorgeous tweeds and real leather brogues.'

'Not just farmers, then. County types really,' said Angie, looking interested. 'Do the Nicholsons treat you as one of the family?'

'Do I meet their friends, do you mean? Sometimes. But usually when they have visitors I eat with the housekeeper. From choice,' she added.

'And Paul? How are you making out with him?'

'All right. He's still on crutches, but his last X-ray showed some bony union.'

Angie rolled her eyes despairingly. 'I don't want a breakdown on his medical condition, you dope! I want a progress report on your personal relationship.'

A tinge of colour came into Linda's cheeks, but she answered calmly enough. 'We get on all right. Most of the time.'

Angie spotted the blush and grinned knowingly. 'And the rest of the time you're quarrelling?'

'He can be a bit difficult.'

'I'll bet. How many times has he kissed you?'

'Patients aren't supposed to kiss their nurses,' Linda said primly, couldn't help laughing at Angie's droll expression, and added between gasps, 'Only once—honestly.'

Angie smiled. 'Once is better than never, I suppose, but why didn't he do it again? Did you tell him off?'

'Of course I did. This conversation's getting very silly, Angie. I have to go now or I'll be late.'

Because she didn't often travel at the rush hour, she had forgotten what it was like. When she arrived at Paul's flat she was tired and dishevelled, her hair blown about by the draught on the Underground corridors, and very conscious of the need to tidy herself up. She turned the front door handle, but the door didn't open. Tom couldn't have arrived yet, for his car was nowhere to be seen, and there were several empty spaces nearby. She put out her hand to ring the bell, then changed her mind. She remembered that the hall floor had been slippery, and that Paul had negotiated it on his crutches with some difficulty. If he had to answer her ring himself, he might fall.

There was a narrow passage at the side of the house. She took it and came to two wooden doors, one of which was locked, the other open. She thought that the unlocked one might lead into the patio at the back of Paul's flat, went down some stone steps and across the paved area. There was a large window at the end of the living-room and the curtains were undrawn. Paul was sitting on the sofa, and beside him a girl. They were enclosed in a circle of light from a tall standard lamp behind them, and they had glasses in their hands. As she stared in at them the girl took the glass from Paul and put it down on a table with her own. Then she leant towards him and put her hands on his shoulders. Seconds later they were kissing, and Linda moved at last, backing away out of the faint light cast by the room, into the shadows at the foot of the steps.

She was shaken, trembling, overcome by the strength of her emotion. Gripped by a jealousy so fierce that it frightened her. If only it could have been her on the sofa! If only she had the self-confidence to initiate a kiss, as that girl had done. They had looked intimate, at ease with each other, so they had made love before. She stumbled up the stone steps and around to the front of the house, just as a car door slammed and Tom appeared at the gate.

'Hallo. I didn't see you come in.'

'I—I've been here a minute or two. I was just trying to decide whether to ring.'

'Door's probably open.'

'No, it isn't.'

Tom tried it, then put a finger on the bell. The door opened and a redhaired girl stood looking out at them. 'You're Tom, aren't you. We've met once or twice. And you're Linda. I've heard a lot about you!'

She was smiling, self-assured, very beautiful. Even Linda, who didn't study the fashion magazines as Angie did, recognised her face. Fenella Freeman, whom the gossip columnists linked quite correctly with Paul. Was she the real reason that he had wanted to come to London? She stood aside to let them pass, and followed them back into the living-room.

Paul was still on the couch. He asked Fenella to pour them drinks. As the girl passed by Linda she gave her a friendly smile.

'Want to freshen up? The cloakroom's by the front door,' thereby reminding Linda how dishevelled she must be, and making it plain how much at home she was in Paul's flat.

Linda bolted herself into the cloakroom. She filled up the basin and splashed water on her face, rubbed vigorously with a towel, stared at herself in the mirror and was surprised to see that she looked no different, in spite of her inward turmoil. She hoped they would be leaving soon and lingered in the cloakroom as long as she could.

She thought it surprising that Fenella hadn't been one of Paul's visitors while he had been in hospital, but perhaps she had been out of the country, for she was a girl who was reported as getting around. Or perhaps she had simply called when Linda was off duty.

Fenella was beside Paul again when Linda returned and Tom was sitting opposite them, unable to remove his eyes from the model girl, totally bemused by her, looking Linda considered, rather foolish. Paul on the other hand was relaxed, stretched out comfortably, laughing easily at Fenella's sallies. Linda would have liked to hate her, but found it difficult. She was so amusing, so irreverent in her attitude to her own fame and fortune. And to Paul's.

Tom had asked some question about the current Grand Prix world champion, and what qualities were needed to win.

Fenella said airily, 'You need a car that doesn't break down and a driver who makes almost no mistakes. Correct, Paul?' She laid a slim hand on his shoulder and rubbed her cheek against his.

She's in love with him, thought Linda, and she doesn't mind who knows it. Paul, on the other hand, gave nothing away. She had learnt after two months in his company that he was not a man who often revealed his feelings. If he loved Fenella in return he wouldn't wear his heart on his sleeve. He was the sort of man who would arrange a quiet wedding to avoid the press photographers.

'Fill yours again, darling?' Fenella leant across him, her red hair swirling across his chest, but he put a hand on top of hers, stopping her. 'No more, Fen! I'm on the wagon. My medical advisers don't recommend excessive consumption, do they, Linda?'

She shook her head and made a valiant attempt at a smile. 'You look as if you could do with another glass,' he went on. 'Had a hectic day?'

'Yes. The shops were packed.' She yawned, simulating fatigue. 'When are we leaving?'

'What's the hurry?' asked Fenella, but Tom, tearing his eyes from the girl with obvious difficulty, brought his attention to bear on his friend, who was also his patient.

'This is very pleasant, but I don't think we should be too late getting back.'

'No problem,' Fenella cut in quickly. 'You two go and we'll follow later.'

Paul laughed. 'Fenella love, how do you think I'd fit into that snappy little two-seater of yours with this?' and he tapped his plastered leg lightly.

'Then I'll borrow someone else's car. Johnny lives just round the corner.'

'Johnny wouldn't trust you with his car, my girl. No, I'll go back with them, but there's no rush. If we leave by eight we'll be home around ten.'

'Then we must have something to eat. Is there much in your kitchen?'

'Nothing fresh. A few tins. The flat hasn't been used since my accident.'

'Okay, darling, we'll pick up some Chinese food. Coming, Linda?' Fenella, though plainly disappointed at not being left alone with Paul, was not a girl who sulked. She turned the oven on, put plates in to heat, rummaged in a cupboard and found a bottle of white wine, slung a coat round her shoulders and led the way out.

While they were waiting in the Chinese restaurant for their food to be packaged, Fenella made idle conversation. It appeared she had met Paul through Anne, with whom she had been at school. 'Though Anne was head girl when I was just a junior. How do you get on with her, by the way?'

'All right,' Linda said cautiously, and Fenella laughed disbelievingly.

'So you say! And Jackie?'

'She can be a bit difficult sometimes.'

'She certainly can, and the situation is not made any easier by the fact that they compete over Paul.'

'Compete? What do you mean?'

'You must have noticed that Jackie has a crush on him, which annoys dear Anne more than it should.

Because,' said Fenella, smiling broadly now, 'she once had a crush on him herself. Or in her case, since she was older, I suppose one could call it love!'

Linda began to feel uncomfortable. 'I don't think you ought to be telling me this, Miss Freeman.' She tried to keep her voice casual, not wanting to give offence.

Fenella stared, then gave her easy laugh. 'Why ever not? Because you live in their house? Aren't you a loyal little thing!'

Beneath the amusement there was a hint of annoyance. She fixed her large blue eyes on Linda, stared at her for a long time in silence, then asked suddenly, 'Does Paul really need a nurse any longer?'

Shades of Anne, thought Linda ruefully, and made much the same reply, that his doctors must think he did. 'A private nurse is expensive. They wouldn't keep me on just for fun.'

'The Nicholsons are loaded,' Fenella retorted, 'so that wouldn't bother them. Perhaps Paul likes having you around.' This last sentence was spoken very softly, and the blue eyes narrowed as she scrutinised the other girl again. 'If you bought some decent clothes you wouldn't be bad-looking,' she allowed. 'Good skin, nice eyes, passable figure.'

So much for the blue suede outfit of which she had been so proud! Linda felt suddenly at the model girl's impertinence. 'Do stop it, Miss Freeman,' she said, controlling herself with difficulty. 'You can't seriously think Paul would be interested in me with you around.' She managed a brief smile. 'You must know that you're absolutely gorgeous. You don't have to worry about the competition.'

Fenella's face relaxed a little. 'Sorry, I didn't mean to offend you. Truth is I'm nothing like as sure of Paul as I appear to be. If he was just a playboy, like some of the other racing drivers, I could handle him better. But he isn't, you see. He has brains and he's educated. And he gets bored easily. Looks aren't enough to hold a man like that.'

Especially if he was in love with another woman, thought Linda, momentarily sorry for Fenella. How difficult relationships were! If only one could fall in love and have one's love reciprocated. Her thoughts were interrupted by the arrival of a waitress with their order in a paper carrier.

The two girls returned to the flat and sat around in the living-room with trays on their knees, eating the delicious food. Somehow the sparkle had gone out of the evening. Fenella was quieter now and Paul had begun to look tired, as he often did by this hour. Linda was relieved when they were once more in Tom's car and speeding down the A21.

Though Paul seemed disinclined to talk, Tom was positively garrulous. 'Terrific girl, Fenella!' He had said the same thing several times over in a variety of different ways. He was obviously badly smitten and longing to discuss her.

Linda was prepared to humour him, and not only out of kindness. She very much wanted to know how important the beautiful model was in Paul's life. 'I don't remember seeing her at the hospital,' she said casually, and turning her head to look at Paul. 'Did she come?'

His eyes were shut and he didn't bother to open them. 'No, she didn't. She was abroad.'

'Working?'

'I suppose so. In the Bahamas, I think, modelling next year's beach wear or some such nonsense.' He sounded rather bad-tempered, and Linda wondered with a pang if he regretted leaving the girl.

# CHAPTER SEVEN

WHEN they arrived at Faversham Court Paul said he was going straight to bed. Anne, who had come into the hall to meet them, asked if they didn't want something to eat.

'We had some Chinese grub at Paul's flat,' said Tom, with his wide disarming smile. 'Fenella Freeman was there,' he added, and his smile widened.

Anne stiffened. 'How did she know you were in town?'

'Because I rang her,' Paul said carelessly, resting a hand for a moment on Linda's shoulder as he fumbled with his crutches. 'I'm tired, Anne. I'm going to bed.'

The only help he would accept nowadays was in getting his shoes off, because his leg injuries made bending difficult. When she had done that Linda left him. 'I'll look in again when you're settled, in case you want anything.'

'I shouldn't bother. All I need is sleep. Goodnight, Linda.' He lay back on the pillow and shut his eyes.

Linda looked for a moment or two at his handsome face, and her heart ached with love for him. It wasn't just physical attraction. It went a lot deeper than that. She had tried to fight it, but she know now that she hadn't succeeded. She felt for him what she had never felt for any other man. She gazed at him sadly, said a quiet goodnight and slipped from the room.

Tom seemed to have gone, and Anne waylaid her in the hall. 'You're looking absolutely bushed, Nurse Mannering. Come and have a drink.'

'Thank you, Mrs Nicholson, but I don't think——'

'Nonsense, my dear.' Anne was more affable than usual. 'Of course you must have one. A medium sherry is your tipple, isn't it?'

James was deep in a book on one side of the fire and only raised his head for long enough to greet her. Jackie wasn't around. Anne sat beside Linda on a sofa and asked how her day had gone. A little surprised by all this attention, Linda answered politely, then it gradually dawned on her what Anne was after. She was probing about Paul and Fenella, how long they had been alone.

'Paul looks so tired. He didn't leave the flat, did he?'

'I wouldn't have thought he could, but I parted from him about eleven, so I don't really know.'

'And what time did you get back?' Anne asked quickly.

'Oh, sixish, I suppose.'

'But who cooked his lunch?'

'He had a friend coming—some man in his racing team.'

'So Fenella came after lunch,' Anne murmured, glanced across at her husband, who hadn't stirred and seemed totally immersed in his book. 'What did you think of her, my dear?'

'She's just about the most beautiful girl I've ever seen,' answered Linda. 'And really quite nice.'

This answer didn't appear to please the other woman. Her lips thinned in the now familiar way. She beat a tattoo on the arm of the sofa. 'That sort of girl causes nothing but trouble. I can't think what Paul sees in her.'

Linda couldn't help smiling. 'I should have thought it was obvious what he sees in her. Tom couldn't stop gawping!' She finished her sherry, thanked Anne politely and said that she was tired too and she wanted to go to bed.

As she crossed the large room, James leant towards his wife and said quietly, 'Don't make it too obvious,

Anne.' Anne gave an angry laugh and started to reply, but what she said was cut off as Linda shut the door quickly.

She climbed the stairs thoughtfully, convinced now that Biddy and Fenella were right—Anne had been in love with Paul, almost certainly still was. Or perhaps it was not so much love any more as the reluctance of a fiercely possessive woman to give up a man who had once been involved with her. If so she was being both foolish and indiscreet. James had heard their conversation, though he hadn't appeared to be listening. He knew what Anne had been getting at and he didn't like it.

Linda's last waking thoughts were that the sooner Paul left this house the better for everyone, including herself. Whether he was to blame for it or not, he was causing heartache and possible damage to quite a few lives.

Next day Paul complained of considerable pain in his left leg, and since he was usually so stoical, Linda guessed that he must be suffering quite acutely. She was worried in case he had damaged it in some way yesterday, but Tom, who came when she called him, could find nothing wrong.

'I think you just overdid it, my dear chap. Take it easy today. Don't go out, and I'll ask Biddy to ease up on the physio.'

By Saturday he was back to normal. It was a cold bright day and the local hunt was out. Paul wanted to watch them set off, so they drove to the next village and parked at the edge of the green. When they saw him, numerous people came up to speak, aristocratic-looking men, bluff farmers, horsey women. There was one girl in particular with a long well-bred face and a very upper-class drawl, which made Linda want to laugh. She noticed the girl because her horse was so beautiful, a glossy chestnut, whose coat shone in the November sunshine. When the girl saw them she dismounted quickly, handed the reins to a young man and strolled over to the car.

'So the rumours were true,' she smiled as Paul rolled his window down. 'You are on the mend.' The words were casually spoken, but her eyes gave her away. She was staring at him avidly, bending towards him, one gloved hand resting on the rim of the window.

'Hallo, Jennifer. Quite a time since we saw each other,' Paul said pleasantly. 'This is Linda Mannering, who looks after me very well.'

Jennifer, after a quick glance at Linda and a most perfunctory nod, concentrated on Paul again. They swapped local gossip, talked about a mutual friend who had recently married, teased one another and laughed a lot.

'I've known Jennifer since she was in her pram,' Paul remarked.

'Yes,' smiled Jennifer. 'Our nannies used to go for walks together! So he's my oldest friend, Miss ... Mannering, was it? I think it's about time I paid you a visit, Paul.'

'Why not?' agreed Paul. 'Any time.'

Someone was calling the girl away. The hunt was beginning to move off. Jennifer touched Paul lightly on the shoulder. 'Anne wasn't exactly welcoming when I last telephoned.'

'Really?' Paul looked surprised, then annoyed. 'I had no idea that you'd rung.' He added slowly, 'She must have forgotten to tell me.'

'Forgot deliberately, I should say,' Jennifer retorted crisply, raising her riding crop and turned away with a cheerful, 'Be seeing you!'

Paul watched her swing into the chestnut's saddle, a frown on his good-looking face. 'Sometimes Anne interferes too much,' he muttered, more to himself than to Linda. 'The sooner I get away from Faversham the better. I knew it was a mistake to come.'

The hunt departed noisily and enthusiastically, and Linda watched them go with mixed feelings. 'I don't really approve of the sport,' she confessed, 'but I have to admit they're a grand sight.'

'If we drive to the top of the hill, we may see them go across the bottom of the valley,' Paul suggested.

So they drove up the hill and parked at the edge of a clearing among some giant beech tress. Paul raked the valley with his binoculars. 'No sign of them.' He had rolled the window down again and the breeze blew his dark hair into his eyes. He brushed it back impatiently and turned awkwardly in his seat, for he had insisted on sitting in the front, and there wasn't much room for his plastered leg. In shifting he loosened his grip on the binoculars, and because he hadn't put the strap round his neck, they fell on to his knees.

He grabbed at them at the same moment as Linda did. She caught them in time before they slid to the floor, and as she straightened their heads were very close together.

'Well caught!' exclaimed Paul, with an approving smile. He didn't move away from her. Instead he took the fieldglasses, dumped them on the back seat and put his hands on her arms. 'You have a very pretty mouth,' he said softly, drew her towards him and kissed her on the lips.

She was too startled to respond. She remained quite immobile under his hands, though her heart started to pound. She thought she stopped breathing. After a few seconds Paul drew back, his expression quizzical.

'Now tell me off again. I'm quite expecting it!'

The colour rushed into her cheeks. She was breathing rapidly now. 'You shouldn't have done that. I told you before that I didn't like it. It's not fair to—to take advantage of the fact that we're alone.'

'Oh, come *on*!' said Paul, beginning to look irritated. He leant back in his seat and closed his eyes. 'It was only a kiss, for God's sake.'

Linda's lips trembled. It would be so easy to throw herself into his arms, to respond with passion to his kisses, but she remembered the scene she had witnessed in his flat and pride came to her rescue. Pride and common sense.

In a cold little voice she told him that nurses didn't get involved with their patients. It just wasn't ethical.

Paul gave a contemptuous snort. 'How you do go on about one kiss!' He sounded bored and bad-tempered. 'What a little prig you are, Linda.'

Hurt by this unkind remark, she flared back at him, 'I'm not a prig! I just don't care to be a sort of substitute, because the girl you really want to make love to isn't available.'

He opened his eyes at that. 'What an extraordinary thing to say. What the hell does it mean?'

She bit her lower lip hard, close to tears now.

'Oh, come on,' he said impatiently, 'you can't make a remark like that without clarifying it.'

She swallowed and said in a small voice, 'I meant Fenella, of course.'

His annoyance evaporated, to be replaced by a look of amusement. 'Funny girl! You don't rate yourself very highly, do you? Why should you think I wouldn't want to kiss you for your own sake?' He stretched out a hand and ran his forefinger over her lips. 'A beautiful mouth,' he said quietly, 'And most definitely kissable!'

His touch and his tone nearly melted her resistance, but the thread of laughter in his voice stiffened her resolve not to give way. Paul was a sophisticated, worldly man, who had probably made love to a lot of women. It would mean nothing to him, but a great deal to her.

She pushed his hand away and in a hard little voice said, 'Stick to Fenella. You'll soon be back in your flat, then she can move in with you.'

The amusement went and he gave her an exasperated look. 'Why the devil are you going on about Fenella? She's just another girl, no one very special.'

'Oh, really?' Her voice rose as she lost control. 'You could have fooled me all right! You certainly seemed to be enjoying yourselves when I arrived back at your flat . . .' Her words tailed off at the look on his face.

'What are you trying to say?' And when she turned her head away, appalled at what she had just blurted out, he put a hand behind it and swung her round to look at him. 'Fenella let you in. You couldn't have seen us—or was that just the product of an overheated imagination?'

The contempt in his voice stung. 'I did see you,' she mumbled. 'I went round to the back because I—I didn't want you to have to come to the front door. I had no idea you had a visitor. I—I wouldn't dream of spying on people like that,' and a tear trickled down her cheek.

He was staring at her very hard. She brushed the tear away, but another followed. She fumbled vainly for her handkerchief and was reduced to sniffing, when she couldn't find it. Paul swore under his breath and gave her his.

'Please stop crying, Linda.' He said the words surprisingly gently.

She blew her nose, feeling ashamed of her loss of control. 'You . . . you do believe me? I really had no idea that Fenella was there.'

'Of course I believe you, my dear girl.' He showed signs of losing patience again. 'You're not the sort who does underhand things. O.K? Shall we go?'

So they left without ever seeing the hunt again and

drove home in silence. As she turned through the stone gates, Linda said in a small voice,' I suppose you think I'm a complete fool?'

He laughed and she cast a quick glance in his direction. His ill humour had completely gone, and he returned her glance with a mixture of amusement and something that was almost tenderness. 'No, I don't think you're a fool, little girl. I should have known better. I forget sometimes how unworldly you are. The girls I know wouldn't react like that to a kiss!'

Nor most of the ones she knew! Angie would probably have been delighted, and not too worried that Paul was her patient.

'It must be that vicarage upbringing,' Paul went on teasingly, and she flushed awkwardly.

The others were all out with the hunt, she had seen them in the distance as they drove off, so there was no one to witness any constraint between them—not that Paul seemed in the least embarrassed. When she joined him for tea he was perfectly at ease. It was she who felt tense.

After a long silence she said suddenly, 'It might be better if I told the Principal Nursing Officer that I want to go back to Queen's. I don't have to stay here.'

He looked astonished. 'My dear Linda, what on earth do you mean?'

Doggedly she tried to explain—that there was bound to be some awkwardness between them, that perhaps it would be easier if he had another nurse.

'Absolute rubbish!' Paul said forcefully. 'If I don't feel awkward why should you? Couldn't you take life a little less seriously, Linda? Hmm?' and he gave her his charming smile.

He thought her gauche and inexperienced. He had called her prim. He quite liked her, but he didn't understand why she had been so upset, which was perhaps just as well. He made it very plain that kissing her had been a momentary whim, which he would under no circumstances repeat. He had got the message: she didn't like casual lovemaking. So from now on she had nothing to fear. He would keep his distance.

The following morning Jennifer Dudley arrived, while Paul was having his physiotherapy. Linda was drinking coffee in the kitchen with Mrs Nelson, and offered to answer the doorbell. Today Jennifer was casually dressed in a sheepskin jacket and fawn trousers.

'Hallo, Nurse.' She stepped into the hall, glancing around as she did so. 'Who's in?' she asked.

'Paul, of course. Mrs Nicholson and Jackie are out.'

'Good!' said Jennifer in that crisp upper-class voice, that sounded affected but probably wasn't. She might well have talked like that as a little girl, Linda thought, hiding a smile. Jennifer had a carrier bag under her arm, stuffed with books. 'Where is he?' she asked.

Linda indicated Paul's room. 'But he's in the middle of his physio session, Miss Dudley. It should be over soon. Would you like some coffee? Mrs Nelson and I were just having a cup.'

'Thanks.' Jennifer strolled across the hall and pushed open the library door, like someone who knew the house well. 'Good, there's a fire. I'll have it in here.'

Linda wasn't sure whether to be irritated or amused by the other girl's attitude. Jennifer quite obviously regarded her as some sort of domestic help. 'Oh well . . .' she thought philosophically, and went back to the kitchen.

When she told Mrs Nelson that Jennifer was expecting her coffee in the library, the housekeeper gave an ominous sniff. 'That one! I'm surprised she hasn't been round before.' She poured a cup out and Linda picked it up.

'I'll take it, Mrs Nelson.'

'That you will not, Miss Mannering. It's no part of your duties.' Mrs Nelson held out a large red hand, and after a moment's hesitation Linda passed the cup to her.

'Poor Mr Paul,' the housekeeper commented, when she returned, and at Linda's enquiring look, 'She's been after him for years!' She sat down heavily, poured second cups for them both and pushed a plate of biscuits towards Linda. 'Stuck at home like he is, he'll find it difficult getting away from her!'

Aware that it wasn't a good thing to gossip, but tempted none the less, Linda remarked with a smile that Mrs Nicholson was more than capable of giving unwelcome visitors the brush-off.

'That she is,' Mrs Nelson agreed. 'She's been doing it ever since he came back.'

Linda couldn't resist asking if it was really true that Paul hadn't been home for five years before his accident. She felt mean as she put the question, because she already knew the answer. What she longed to know and didn't like to ask was exactly why he had stayed away.

Mrs Nelson nodded vigorously. 'Yes, Nurse, I'm afraid it's true. Poor Mr James was that upset! If you ask me it was a bad day when he married Mrs Nicholson—and to think it was his brother who introduced them!'

This rather involved speech seemed to corroborate what other people had said. Linda stared at the housekeeper, uncertain whether to ask what she meant, and decided against it. Mrs Nelson had no such reservations, apparently.

'Things might have been different if Mr Paul's mother hadn't married again. But she did, and she doesn't take much interest in them now. Can you credit it? Didn't even fly over to see him when he was so ill.'

'I think they didn't want to alarm her,' said Linda.

'She couldn't have got there in time if—if he'd really been going to die.' Her voice wavered on the words. The thought of what might have happened was truly appalling. 'And afterwards it wasn't necessary.'

'Not necessary!' exclaimed Mrs Nelson. 'Wouldn't you have wanted to see your son if he was ill in hospital? No, she never cared a rap for her sons—more taken up with her social life. Is it any wonder that he turned out the way he did?'

'James doesn't seem to have been affected,' Linda commented, and added quickly, 'Mr James Nicholson,' for Mrs Nelson was nearly as great a stickler for the correct social usage as her employer.

'But they're different, aren't they? the older woman pointed out. 'Mr James hasn't much imagination.'

It was at that moment that Biddy came into the kitchen. 'Paul's free. He'd like some coffee.'

As Linda crossed the hall with the tray, Jennifer appeared at the library door. 'Can I go in now?' Without waiting for an answer she followed Linda into the room and gave Paul a wide smile.

'I've brought you some paperbacks. Hope you haven't read them all.' She emptied the contents of her bag on to a table.

Paul thanked her and Jennifer pulled a chair forward.

'Do you need anything?' Linda asked her patient.

He shook his head and Jennifer said airily, 'If he does I'll let you know. You are going to leave the poor man in peace, I hope?'

Irritated though she was by the other girl's manner, Linda tried not to show it. She answered quietly that there was nothing more to do for her patient, and made for the door.

In the kitchen Biddy and Mrs Nelson were regaling each other with gossip. 'Dear Anne won't be pleased,' Biddy announced gleefully. 'About Jumping Jennifer,' she added for Linda's benefit.

'Why do you call her that?'

'Because she's crazy about show-jumping—pretty good at it too. Compensation for a hopeless love, Tom says!'

'You mean . . .'

'Yes, I do,' Biddy grinned, finished her coffee and rose. 'What a bunch of old women we are! Goodbye, Mrs Nelson, and thanks for the coffee.'

On the way to her car she added thoughtfully, 'Jennifer hasn't a chance against girls like Fenella Freeman. I don't believe Paul thinks of her as anything more than a childhood friend.'

'They seemed very fond of each other, when they met yesterday at the start of the hunt.'

'Only because they've known each other since the year dot,' Biddy commented. 'But she's too much like Anne, poor girl. For Paul I should think it's once bitten, twice shy.'

She laughed and got into her car. When she had driven off, Linda walked round the side of the house and through into the rose garden. She sat on a stone seat and stared rather disconsolately at the freshly pruned roses. She regretted already that she had listened so willingly to gossip. She remained confused and uncertain about Paul's affairs, which perhaps served her right for being so nosy, for asking questions that were none of her business. She wished quite desperately that she had never come to Faversham Court, that she had never met Paul or Anne, or any of the family.

There was the sound of a car coming up the drive. Anne, perhaps? She sat on, although the November air was chilly and the stone was cold on her legs. When she rose at last and went into the house, she heard raised voices in Paul's room and halted outside his door, not liking to intrude.

'Are you going to let her talk to me like that?' Anne asked shrilly, and Paul's reply came quietly.

'For God's sake, you two! Stop being so silly!'

There were a few moments of silence, then the door swung open and Jennifer appeared, her colour high. 'If you have any sense, Paul,' she flung over her shoulder, 'you'll get out of this house as soon as you're able!'

She stalked past Linda without a word, wrenched open the front door and slammed it behind her. Astounded, Linda remained where she was until Jennifer had driven off. Then, suddenly conscious of having been an eavesdropper, however unintentionally, she started to move quietly towards the stairs. Unfortunately Anne, after a few subdued words to Paul, came out of his room and saw her.

Whereas Jennifer's cheeks had been fiery red, Anne's were very pale. Her hands were tightly clenched. Her expression was bleak. 'Oh, it's you, Nurse,' she said edgily. 'I suppose you heard what that dreadful girl said?'

'I'm afraid I couldn't help it, Mrs Nicholson. I was right outside the door——'

Anne cut her short. 'All right! All right! Just don't let her see Paul again under any circumstances. You shouldn't have admitted her.'

'Linda!' Paul's voice was louder than usual. He sounded angry and exasperated.

'You'd better go in,' Anne said thinly. 'Do your best to calm him down.'

Linda went into the room and found that he had half risen from his chair, got entangled in his crutches, and was grasping the arm of the chair to stop himself from falling. She steadied him and he sank back on to the seat, letting out a long frustrated sigh.

'Why the hell did you stay away so long?' he asked disagreeably.

'I thought you wanted to be left alone.'

He rested his head against the back of the chair and stared up at the ceiling. 'With Jennifer? My God!' He gave an irritable laugh. 'She frightens the life out of me!'

'I don't believe that.'

He looked at her sharply and scowled when he saw her smile. 'It isn't funny, my girl. I prefer women who let me make the passes!'

Her smile broadened. 'Well, I think it serves you right. A sort of poetic justice for being so fascinating! But why was Mrs Nicholson so annoyed?'

His mouth twisted. 'Because she found us in a clinch.'

'But you just said——'

'Jennifer was kissing *me*,' he said ungallantly, and with the air of a man at the end of his tether.

'And Mrs Nicholson didn't like that?' The words were out before she could stop them.

He gave a hard angry laugh. 'They've never liked each other. So Anne made one of her snide remarks and Jennifer lost her temper. Women! Dear God, how tired I am of domesticity. How I long to be back in my own place!'

A week passed and Jennifer didn't call again. Then one morning Paul dropped a bombshell at her feet when she took in his breakfast. He still ate it in bed, though he was up by ten these days. She propped up his pillows, swung the bed-table across his knees and laid the tray on it. Then she poured his first cup of coffee and retreated to a seat by the radiator with her own.

'I've been thoroughly spoilt,' he remarked, smiling across at her. 'I shan't like doing things for myself.' This didn't seem to call for an answer. After a few moments he went on, 'I've decided to go back to London. It's Thursday today. I shall move on Monday.'

Linda's lips parted, but no words came. She had always known that it would happen one day, but hadn't expected it so soon. And she hadn't expected to feel quite such despair.

'You look surprised, Linda.'

'I'm ... wondering how you'll manage. Shopping ... cleaning the flat.'

'I've always had a cleaning woman, a middle-aged widow who will be delighted to come in for longer hours. I've already telephoned her about it. And when she can't—well, I'm not short of friends.'

Girl-friends, he meant. She made a business of buttering a piece of toast. 'And physio?'

'There are plenty of private physiotherapists in London.'

'Yes, of course. I shall be quite glad to go back to proper nursing.'

His mouth curved sardonically. 'I believe you. You haven't been too happy lately, have you? Anne been getting on your nerves? Or young Jackie?' She didn't answer. He frowned and put his coffee cup down with a bang. 'Or is it me, Linda? Well, you won't have to put up with me for much longer.'

There was a good deal of resistance to Paul's decision, especially from Anne. He told them that evening when they were having coffee in the drawing room after dinner.

Anne's hand shook so that she spilt coffee on her skirt. She dabbed at it crossly. 'You must be mad even to think of it! James, tell him he mustn't go.' However, she gave her husband no time to comment, hurrying on with an endless list of questions. What if he had an accident? What about the hours when his cleaning woman wasn't there? Why couldn't he stay on with them? Was he bored with them already?

James, when appealed to again by Anne, was inclined

to be equivocal. He saw her point, but if Paul had made up his mind——

'I have,' said his brother quietly.

Linda was sitting back from the others, not wanting to intrude on this family discussion. Anne, who usually ignored her, glanced at the girl now and tried to enlist her support. 'You agree with me, don't you, Nurse Mannering? It's quite impossible for him to leave. He's been very ill and he still needs attention.'

'I'm afraid he's made up his mind, Mrs Nicholson. I think you're just wasting your time trying to change it.' Anne's mouth compressed angrily and her cheeks were tinged with pink, so Linda hurried on. 'Honestly, he'll be all right. He's within two or three miles of Q.C.H. He has a G.P. in Hampstead and lots of friends.'

'So drop it, Anne dear,' Paul suggested, pleasantly but firmly. 'There are good reasons for my wanting to go back—among them that I have to start thinking of the future. I shall be more in touch with people in London.'

Anne never gave up easily. 'And how will you get about?'

'Taxis. Or friends.' He was beginning to look irritated by her persistence.

James, who had contributed little to the discussion, asserted himself for once and told his wife to leave well alone. It was up to his brother to decide. She was not to interfere.

Jackie had been out that evening, but when she heard the news she appeared to be even more upset than Anne. She went around with a face of deepest gloom, struck attitudes, sulked and was more difficult than ever. As Biddy said with a grin, that meant that she was absolutely awful!

The young physiotherapist had come in for her last session with Paul on the Saturday morning. The two girls were saying goodbye to each other and making plans to meet in the future.

'How's dear Anne taking it?' Biddy asked in a low voice as they stood on the drive by her car.

'She's not pleased,' Linda replied, which was something of an understatement.

Anne's face was taut with disapproval every time Paul's impending departure was mentioned. Her temper, never very reliable, would flare at the least thing, so that Mrs Nelson kept out of her way and advised Linda to do the same.

On Sunday morning Linda was in Paul's room, helping him to run through the routine exercises Biddy had given him, when there was a sharp rap on the door.

Anne came in, looking displeased. 'Does he really need to do his exercises on a Sunday? I have a lot to talk about.'

'Sunday's like any other day to a patient,' Linda answered politely but firmly. 'Biddy says it's most important not to miss even one.'

'And who will keep him up to the mark when he's in London?' Anne riposted.

Paul sighed and rolled his trouser leg down. 'Anne dear, don't let's go through all that again.'

'I can't help it!' Anne exclaimed, her voice choked with emotion. 'Paul, please, please won't you reconsider?'

'No, my dear,' he said gently, and Anne gave a jerky sob. Paul cast a quick look at Linda. 'Would you leave us alone for a few minutes, please.'

Embarrassed by Anne's rapidly slipping control, Linda was only too glad to leave the room. She had coffee with Mrs Nelson, took a stroll around the garden and wondered when she should rejoin Paul. Coming back through the conservatory she walked into Anne, who was cutting back the geraniums. The older woman looked quite different, relaxed, happy, almost smug, so whatever Paul had said to her had done the trick. Linda was astonished by the change in her, but also relieved. It would make her last day at Faversham Court a reasonably pleasant one.

That evening Tom came in to say goodbye to his old friend, and to urge him not to do anything foolish. When he was leaving he asked Linda to see him out.

'Glad to be going back to London?' he asked, halting by the front door.

The others were in the drawing room and the television was on, so she felt free to speak without being overheard. 'Yes, I am. Very, very glad!'

Tom looked surprised at her fervour and subjected her to a critical professional stare, as if she was one of his patients. 'You're looking peaky. It can't be overwork.'

'Of course not.'

'Then what is it?' She tried to brush aside his question, but Tom wouldn't be put off. 'When a girl has dark circles under her eyes and obviously isn't sleeping, there's a common enough explanation. I wonder if it's the correct one.'

'Oh, Tom, do drop it!'

'And the explanation's usually quite simple. You've been missing some man. I thought you told me there was no one special.'

'There isn't Tom. Truly,' Linda said with an unconscious wistfulness that made the young doctor look at her very thoughtfully.

'All right, Linda, I believe you. Goodbye, then. I'll be in touch.' He dropped a light kiss on her cheek and left.

Nice, ordinary, uncomplicated Tom, who had made it very plain over the past few weeks that he was strongly attracted to her. If only, she thought sadly, it could have been Tom with whom she had fallen in love, how much easier life would have been.

# CHAPTER EIGHT

ON Monday morning Linda was up very early to help Paul with his final preparations. It had been agreed that Anne was to drive him to London, and Jackie announced at the last moment that she was going with them. Linda had already telephoned Queen's College Hospital and spoken to one of Miss Cameron's deputies. She had been asked to report to the office at two o'clock that afternoon.

They left Faversham Court just after ten. James came out to see them off, gripped his brother by the shoulder and wished him well. He shook hands with Linda, gave the slow kindly smile that lit up his heavy face, and thanked her warmly for all her help. She sat in the back of the car with Jackie. Glancing out of the rear window, for a last view of the old house, she caught a sad look on James' face and wondered if he was going to miss Paul very much.

Jackie was effervescent today, a changed girl from the sulky creature of the weekend—in one of her half friendly moods, inclined to be pitying, because Linda was returning to the hard slog of hospital life.

'Don't be patronising, my girl,' Paul said sharply. 'I doubt if you'll ever have a job that's half as worthwhile as Linda's.'

Jackie flushed angrily and relapsed into silence. Anne always talked less than usual when driving, and Paul contented himself with the occasional remark. Linda sat directly behind him and stared at the back of his head, at the thick dark hair that curled slightly over his collar, at the strong profile when he turned his head to look

out of the window. This might be the last time that she
ever saw him, unless he invited her round to his flat. A
courtesy invitation, perhaps, a thank-you for her care
of him. Or she supposed that she might meet him some
day in a shop or a theatre. Might! The likelihood wasn't
very great.

Tom and Biddy, when they had said their goodbyes,
had both talked about keeping in touch. Tom had asked
if she would be free next week on his half day, but
Linda had explained that she would not know her off
duty times until she was assigned to her new post. If
only it had been Paul trying to fix up a meeting as soon
as possible. Her eyes filled with tears. She stared out of
the window blindly and wiped them away with the back
of her hand. Turned back, and saw to her dismay that
Anne was watching her in the driving mirror. Did the
older woman guess her secret? If she did it made no
odds now.

The original plan was that they should drive to Paul's
flat, and that Linda would leave from there. The
Underground ran from Hampstead to a station very
near Q.C.H. Anne said suddenly, 'There's really no
point your coming on to Paul's place, Nurse Mannering.
We'll drop you at the hospital on the way.'

So when they crossed Waterloo Bridge Anne turned
in the direction of Trafalgar Square, and a quarter of
an hour later drew into the kerb outside the nurses'
home.

'Is this where you live? Rather drab, isn't it?'

The home was a red brick Victorian building, strictly
functional, begrimed with decades of London soot.
Linda was so used to it that she hardly noticed its appearance normally, but she could see that to outsiders it
might look rather forbidding.

'It's quite comfortable inside,' she said, fumbled with
the door catch and got out. Anne followed her and

unlocked the boot. Linda took out her case and her
canvas grip, fought hard to control her emotions and
walked back round the car to Paul's side. He had rolled
down his window and was looking up at her. She knew
every curve of his handsome face, every hollow. She
knew how he looked when he was sleeping, when he
was teasing her, when he was bored or annoyed. A nurse
learns a great deal about her patient if she stays with
him for three months.

She swallowed on the lump in her throat and held out
her hand. As he took it in a firm clasp she said lightly,
'Goodbye, Paul. I hope things go well for you. I expect
I shall hear how you do.'

She would have turned away then, but Paul kept her
hand in his, and stared intently up at her. A faint smile
touched his mouth. 'I expect you will, Linda. Goodbye,'
and he let her go.

Jackie waved carelessly and Linda waved in return.
Anne stood with one hand on the driver's door.
'Goodbye, Nurse Mannering. Thank you for your help.'
Formal to the end. Not once had she said Linda. She
gave the familiar perfunctory smile that was barely more
than a twitch of the lips, and slid gracefully into the car.

Linda bent and picked up her luggage, ran up the
wide steps of the nurses' home and in through the door,
without looking back.

Some girls in the hall exclaimed on seeing her, 'Linda!
You're back!'

She brushed past them blindly and rushed up the
stairs to her room. There was a lift, but she didn't wait
for it, because that would have meant she would have
had to talk to those girls. She was panting by the time
she reached the fourth floor, and her hand trembled so
much she could hardly fit her key into the lock. She
stumbled into the sanctuary of her room, shut the door,
let down the catch and collapsed face down on her bed.

She lay there for a long time, despairing, her face wet with tears. If only she could have said goodbye with no one else around! A proper goodbye, not those few casual words. If only he had said something about seeing her again, given her some faint hope even that he would like to see her. He had kissed her, after all, and told her that she had a beautiful mouth, so he must find her reasonably attractive.

Oh, stop it, stop it! she thought. He had been bored that afternoon, in need of distraction. There were plenty of girls he would rather kiss than her, now that he was back in London.

She had no appetite, so she skipped lunch. At a quarter to two she washed her face, did her hair and put on the little white cap that she hadn't worn while she was with the Nicholsons. It was the Principal Nursing Officer's deputy who saw her, and told her of her new appointment—Male Orthopaedics. Linda accepted this news with indifference. She would have preferred her old ward, but seemed unable to feel anything much, apart from the pain of her separation from Paul.

The deputy, who had only recently been appointed and had been in charge of the Accident Department when Linda worked there, gave her a searching look. 'Aren't you well, Staff Nurse? You usually have a good colour.'

'I'm all right, Miss Armstrong. A bit tired, perhaps.'

'Tired? I hadn't gathered your work was exactly arduous.' The Number Seven had a dry manner.

Linda's mouth twitched. She couldn't face any more probing. 'I—I didn't sleep very well last night.' And that was certainly true. She had lain awake for hours, thinking about Paul.

'Then get up late tomorrow,' Miss Armstrong said more kindly. 'You won't be starting on your new ward until Friday. Go and see Sister now and find out what time she wants you to come on duty.' She smiled and turned back to her paper work.

Sister on Orthopaedics told Linda to come on duty at two o'clock next Friday. She walked slowly back to the nurses' home, made a sudden decision and telephoned her parents. They were delighted when she told them she was coming home for a few days, less delighted when they saw her.

'You don't look well, darling,' her mother said.

'Perhaps I'm cooking a cold,' Linda answered untruthfully, and went to bed early at her mother's suggestion.

It took her a long time to get to sleep, and she didn't wake until ten, when her mother brought her breakfast in bed. Mrs Mannering loved spoiling her hardworking daughter, but Linda would seldom allow her to do so.

The few days passed slowly, draggingly, although she tried to fill them with small tasks. A trip into the nearest town to return library books for her mother, gardening, cake making for the Women's Institute tea. In the evenings she looked up old friends with whom she had been at school. In the past she had been perfectly happy with these simple activities, but that had been before she fell in love. Now she spent most of her time thinking about Paul, and tortured herself wondering who was with him. Fenella? Some other girl? She would never know, for she no longer had any part in his life.

On her last evening at home Mrs Mannering had to attend a governors' meeting at the local secondary school. Linda sat with her father in the cosy, shabby sitting-room and talked about a dozen different things. They had a lot in common and they were very close, so that she wasn't altogether surprised when her father asked suddenly, 'What's wrong, darling? Would you care to tell me?'

She was hunched up on the leather pouffe in front of

a blazing log fire. She looked up at him, where he stood at one end of the mantelpiece, tapping out his pipe into an ashtray.

'No, Daddy. It wouldn't do any good.'

The rector wasn't a man to probe, even if it was his own daughter. He respected the need for privacy. He said gently, 'If you ever do want to talk about it I'm quite a good listener.'

Linda's eyes filled with tears. 'I know, Daddy. Some day perhaps, but not yet,' and she walked quickly out of the room, leaving her father staring after her with a very worried expression on his thin, distinguished face.

It was a relief to start work next day. She knew two of the girls on the male orthopaedic ward, so she settled down quite easily. She had a quick tea in the canteen, met several of her friends and went back on the ward until the night staff came on.

There was a boy of eighteen who was causing them a good deal of worry, with injuries nearly as bad as Paul's had been, though he had been riding a motor bicycle and not a racing car. Linda spent most of the time with him, for he had only just been transferred from the Intensive Care Unit and needed constant attention.

When she went off duty at eight she felt very tired. She was walking through the entrance hall of the nurses' home when Angie called after her.

'Letter for you, Linda!' and she handed it to her friend.

Linda had forgotten to look in the rack when she came back from her leave. She glanced at the writing on the envelope, writing which was surely familiar? She had taken letters of Paul's to the post quite often. The postmark was a London one.

Her hand trembled and she told herself not to be a fool. If it was from Paul, and perhaps she was mistaken, it must be a formal thank you for nursing him. The sort of polite and appreciative letter she had received many times in the past.

She went on staring at it, and Angie stared at her. 'What's wrong? Do you think it's bad news?'

'Oh no! No!' She opened the letter quickly. It was from Paul:

'I rang the nurses' home on Monday evening, but they said you were away until Friday. Please ring me as soon as possible,' and he gave her his telephone number.

'All right?' Angie asked after an anxious look at her friend's set face.

Could he be ill? Wanting her to nurse him again? Had his cleaning woman backed out and he needed help with the shopping? Perhaps it was already too late, and some other girl was undertaking chores that she would willingly have done.

'Excuse me, Angie, I have to phone.'

The telephone box across the hall was occupied, so because she couldn't bear to wait she walked over to the main hospital. There were two there and one was free, but Paul's number was engaged. She put the receiver down and tried again a minute or two later. And again. In the end she got through, but a woman's voice answered—a pretty husky voice that sounded familiar. Fenella, she thought.

'Paul asked me to ring. Linda Mannering.'

'Hi, Linda.' The voice became cool. 'Fenella here. I'll put you through to Paul.'

He came on the line a few seconds later and Linda's hand clenched tightly on the receiver. 'I got your letter,' she said. 'Is there something you want me to do?'

'Do?' He sounded puzzled. 'Just to come round. I miss your solemn little face.' He spoke lightly, teasingly, but his words warmed her heart. He wanted to see her. He had missed her

'When?' she asked, and he said as soon as possible. When was she free?

She had a split duty on Saturday and was free from twelve till four. 'Come to lunch then,' he suggested. 'Can you manage that?'

'Yes, of course.' She made no effort to keep the eagerness out of her voice. Angie, who believed in playing hard to get, would have been horrified if she could have heard. 'But what about food, Paul? How will you manage?'

'You can do the cooking,' he said, and she knew that he was smiling. 'You told me you liked cooking, I remember. I've enough to feed a regiment. Anne went quite wild. How are you, little one? Glad to be back at Queen's?'

'Oh yes!' Glad to be back in London. Overjoyed that she would be seeing him tomorrow. Uncaring that Fenella was with him tonight. Hadn't he said that Fenella was just another girl? If he had only wanted to say thank you he would have done it in some other way—taken her out to dinner when he was more mobile, sent her flowers or chocolates. You didn't ask a girl to your flat and suggest she cooked for you, unless you really liked her.

Linda went to bed that night in a state of complete euphoria, and slept better than she had done for weeks. In the morning she leapt out on to her bedside mat and danced over to the window. A pale winter sun was struggling through the mist that hung over the trees in Regent's Park. It was very cold, but she scarcely noticed it. She was already trying to decide what she would wear when she visited Paul.

# CHAPTER NINE

In the end she decided on fawn corduroy trousers and a chunky Arran sweater, knitted for her last birthday by her mother. It wouldn't do to dress up for a casual lunch. She laid the clothes out on her bed so that she could change at speed, anxious to reach Paul's place as soon as possible. For once her mind was not wholly on her work, so that Sister spoke sharply a couple of times, and looked as if she wasn't very impressed by her new staff nurse.

At twelve Linda couldn't get through the ward doors fast enough. When she was walking along College Street towards Marylebone Road and the Underground, she decided on a sudden impulse to take a taxi. One was cruising by, so she hailed it and arrived at Paul's house perhaps thirty minutes earlier than she might otherwise have done. She pressed the bell below his name-plate and waited with mounting excitement.

The door swung open and there he was, crutches under his elbows, a welcoming smile on his handsome face. She had meant to play it cool, but the smile she gave him in return was dazzling.

'Come in,' he said, and moved rather awkwardly to one side.

She shut the door and they stood for a few seconds in the pleasant spacious hall, staring at each other in silence. Linda's heart was beating rapidly and her legs began to tremble in a most disconcerting way.

'Thank you for coming,' he said quietly. 'I've missed you, little one, more than I can say.' The smile had gone now and he looked very serious. He made a movement towards her, one of his crutches slipped slightly and he swore under his breath. 'I can't wait to get rid of these damn things. Perhaps next week when I see old Charles. They're X-raying me again then, so let's hope for the best.'

She walked before him into the sitting-room, her heart hammering against her chest, overjoyed to be with him and quite sure of one thing. He had wanted to take her in his arms in the hall. He would have done so if he hadn't been hampered by the crutches. A smile trembling on her lips she sat down on the sofa.

'I didn't expect you so soon,' remarked Paul. 'Can I pour you a drink, Linda? Sherry?'

'I don't usually drink at midday——'

'Yes, I remember, but this is a special occasion. We're celebrating my return to London, and the fact that you're no longer nursing me.' There was a gleam in his eyes as he said this, that brought the colour to her cheeks.

'Is that a reason to celebrate?' she asked demurely, and he grinned across at her.

'Of course.' He had lowered himself on to the chair by the drinks table and was filling two glasses. 'Be a good girl and come and get them.'

He followed her back to the couch. She sat down and when he was beside her, handed him his Scotch. 'You once told me it was unethical for a nurse to get involved with her patient. But you're not my nurse now, Linda.'

His dark eyes held hers, intent, questioning. He was not going to kiss her this time unless he was sure she wanted it. She leant a little towards him, magnetised by his stare and by the pull of extreme physical attraction.

'Oh, Paul,' she whispered, 'I've missed you so terribly.'

He took the glass of sherry from her hand and put it down on the low table beside the sofa with his own.

'We'll drink later,' he said softly, and pulled her into his arms.

This time she didn't resist him, responding eagerly to his kisses, running her fingers through his thick dark hair, clinging to him as if she never wanted to let him go. It was Paul who drew back first.

'Well, well!' he observed, looking momentarily disconcerted. 'Is it possible I was mistaken about you, Linda? Someone certainly taught you how to kiss!'

Flushed and dishevelled, she moved away from him, astounded by her own loss of control. 'I've never kissed anyone else like that. Honestly, Paul!'

Something sparked in his eyes for a moment. The cynical look went, to be replaced by an expression of tenderness. 'Dear girl, it's unwise to say things like that to a man.'

'Why not if it's true?'

He ran the tip of one finger down her smooth young cheek. 'You're very sweet. And refreshingly honest.' He reached for her drink and handed it to her, then clinked his own glass against hers. 'Here's to you, sweetheart, and may you always stay the same.'

'Did you really ring me on Monday?' Linda asked, and he nodded.

'I rang the nurses' home and they told me you'd gone away. But no one knew where.'

'I wouldn't have gone if I'd thought you would be getting in touch. Only when we said goodbye . . .' She shut her eyes for a moment, remembering the anguish of that parting. 'You seemed so . . . indifferent.'

He smiled. 'I wasn't going to fix up a meeting in front of Anne and Jackie. I never thought you'd dash off the way you did.'

'I had a horrible three days. Usually I love going home.' She finished her sherry, moved along the sofa

and rested her head against his shoulder. 'Oh, Paul, I'm
so happy!'

His arm slid round her. 'Are you sweetheart? When
I'm free of this cursed plaster, when I'm back to normal
again, we'll have a lot of fun.'

She twisted in his arms so that she could see his face.
'What sort of fun?' she asked doubtfully. 'I'm not a—a
night club sort of girl.' She was remembering his reputation for high living in the capitals of the world.

Paul looked down at her with a frown. 'You don't
credit me with much discrimination, do you, my dear?
I'm well aware that your idea of fun is not Fenella's.
But you do like going to theatres and concerts, don't
you?'

'When I can afford them,' she admitted candidly. 'Or
when someone takes me,' she added with a mischievous
smile. 'Tom was suggesting that we do a show next
week.'

His frown deepened. 'Ah yes, Tom. You like him
quite a lot, don't you?' His voice was casual, but his
manner was not.

Was it possible, could it possibly be true that he was
jealous? She dismissed the idea as ridiculous. She must
have imagined that he minded. 'Yes, I do like him,' she
agreed. 'He and Biddy were very nice to me when I was
at Faversham.'

He finished off his Scotch. 'When shall we eat? You're
not offended at my asking you to cook?'

She gave him a loving smile. 'Of course not. Any
time,' and then wished she hadn't said it, because he
might think her pushy.

She was relieved when he smiled back at her. 'I may
take you up on that. What would you like? An omelette?
Steak? Take your pick.'

'I make quite a good omelette. Stay where you are,
Paul.'

The kitchen was modern and well equipped. She took eggs from the refrigerator and mushrooms from the cold box. While the mushrooms were frying she soaked a lettuce and gazed dreamily out of the window, humming gently to herself. She was so happy that she could have danced around the room. She was alone with Paul because he wanted her to be. He had missed her as much as she had missed him, but—and suddenly she sobered, feeling the first chill of uncertainty—he had not said that he loved her yet.

She beat the eggs, added pepper and salt and tipped them into the pan. It was early days. She must not be impatient. Some time he would say it. Some time he would realise that she wasn't 'just another girl', as he had called poor Fenella. She would make him realise it by the strength of her love for him.

They ate at the kitchen table and Paul wanted to open a bottle of wine, but Linda wouldn't let him. 'I shouldn't be fit for work,' she smiled, so he poured her a glass of lager.

It was a happy relaxed meal. When they were drinking coffee Paul told her that Hugh Mansel was coming round. 'Some time after two. You don't mind, do you? I'd fixed it before I knew you were coming.' He sounded very regretful and Linda's heart lifted joyfully.

He didn't want to share her with someone else. He would have preferred to be alone with her. 'Of course I don't mind. I like Hugh very much.'

They were still at the table when the doorbell rang. Linda opened it and smiled at Hugh. He had a briefcase under one arm and was wearing a dark suit, so that he looked like a city worker. He showed surprise for a moment, then he smiled at her very warmly.

'Hallo, Miss Mannering. This is an unexpected pleasure.'

He followed her into the living-room, but wouldn't sit down. 'I didn't realise you had another visitor, Paul. Shall I come back this evening?'

Paul took Linda's hand and pulled her on to the sofa beside him. 'Of course not, my dear chap. Linda doesn't mind, and she has to get back to the hospital before long.' He slid an arm round her waist, holding her close. 'You can come back this evening,' he said softly, and flicked her hair out of her eyes.

The intimate little gesture, the way he spoke in front of his friend, made her suddenly shy. Colour flooded her face and she wriggled out of his arms. 'You talk to Mr Mansel. I'll do the dishes.'

'The name's Hugh,' Mansel said with a smile. 'May I call you Linda?'

She nodded. In the hall she remembered the dirty glasses, and was about to return for them when Hugh spoke. 'That's a very nice girl, Paul. I didn't expect to find her here.'

'Didn't you, Hugh?' Paul's voice was unusually sober. 'I suppose you think she's too good for me?'

'Much too good, old chap,' Hugh agreed with a little laugh, 'but you always have had the luck of the devil.'

It was only then that Linda realised she was eavesdropping, and suddenly ashamed, moved quietly into the kitchen. It was all part of this wonderful, unexpected thing that had happened to her, Paul's best friend accepting her and making it very plain that he approved.

She was drying the silver when the doorbell sounded again. 'I'll go,' she called, and crossed the hall to open the door. Jackie stood there, wearing a short white fur coat and tight black trousers. She had dumped a couple of bulging carrier bags on the step beside her. Her reaction was even more marked than Hugh's had been, and decidedly less agreeable.

After a few seconds of astonished silence she said sharply, 'What are *you* doing here?'

Linda was too happy to be upset by the other girl's rudeness. 'Paul asked me to lunch,' she said blithely. 'He's in the living-room.'

Jackie gave a most unladylike snort and pushed past her, then came to an abrupt halt when she saw Hugh. The two men were sitting opposite each other, with the contents of Hugh's briefcase spread on a table between them—typewritten notes, engineering blueprints, one or two photographs of racing cars. They were deeply engrossed and didn't look up until Jackie spoke. 'Hallo, Paul. Hallo, Hugh. Am I interrupting something?' She smiled winningly, dropped down beside Paul on the sofa and kissed him on the cheek.

Paul riffled the papers in his hands and Hugh looked quickly at Linda. To see how she was taking Jackie's kiss? Linda didn't regard the younger girl as any sort of threat, so she smiled back at him.

'We are interrupting you,' she said quickly. 'I have to get back to work, so I think I'll go now, Paul.' She diidn't mind leaving him because she knew she would be back soon. Hadn't he asked her to come back that evening? If he didn't say anything now he would probably ring the nurses' home.

She picked up her coat and her shoulder bag. Paul asked what time she was free and when she told him, said that he would telephone after eight. Linda was very conscious of the other two's interest in this exchange. Hugh looked benign, but Jackie made little effort to hide her pique.

'I'm staying in London for a few days,' she told Paul, 'so I think I'll come back some other time when you're not so busy. Anne asked me to bring some things for you,' and she gestured towards the carrier bags.

'Not more food, I hope,' smiled Paul. 'You do that

Jackie, but ring beforehand. I might be out.'

The girl nodded, tossed back her long hair and buttoned up her fur coat. 'Perhaps I could give you a lift, Linda?' she suggested. 'I'm going to Islington, so it wouldn't be much out of my way.'

Rather surprised by this friendly gesture, Linda thanked her, and Paul looked pleased.

'That's kind of you, my dear. Less tiring for the girl than the Underground.'

'And we all know what a strenuous life she leads,' murmured Jackie, as she followed Linda out of the room.

This little dig should have warned Linda of what was to come, but she was still in the state of total euphoria that seemed to have been with her all day, and hardly registered what the other girl had said. Jackie's mini was parked a short way down the street.

'What time are you due at the hospital?' she asked as they drew away from the kerb.

'I'm on duty at four. I'd like to be at the nurses' home by a quarter to, so that I can change.' Linda glanced at her watch. 'There's plenty of time.'

'Good, because I want to talk to you. That's why I came away from Paul's place.'

'Oh!' Linda looked at her companion's taut profile, filled with sudden uneasiness. 'What about?'

'Later,' snapped Jackie. 'Not while I'm driving,' and indeed the traffic on Haverstock Hill was heavy and needed all her attention.

She cut through back streets until she reached the Primrose Hill area, found a parking place and turned off the ignition. Then she swung round in her seat and gave Linda a hard stare. All pretence at friendliness had gone. She looked furious and when she spoke her voice had an edge to it.

'All right, Nurse Mannering. What exactly are you up to?'

Linda was determined not to quarrel with the other girl. It could do no good and would be horribly undignified. She said quietly that she wasn't up to anything. What was Jackie talking about?

'Don't play the innocent!' Jackie spat out. 'I'm talking about you and Paul. I don't believe he asked you to lunch. More likely you invited yourself, and he was too kind to refuse.'

'I wouldn't dream of inviting myself, but if you don't believe me it's just too bad.' Her quiet controlled voice seemed to drive Jackie to fresh anger.

Colour high, the girl told Linda that she was wasting her time chasing Paul. The competition was too fierce. She just wasn't his type.

These spiteful words made little impression on Linda, because she remembered the welcoming look on Paul's face when she had first arrived, the strength of his arms and the tenderness of his kisses. She smiled to herself, and Jackie nearly choked with exasperation.

'You think you're very clever, don't you? Oh, sure, Paul may be making a play for you at the moment—I suppose I have to believe that, because he did say that he'd ring you this evening.' She gave a great shuddering sigh, relapsed into silence and fumbled in the glove compartment for cigarettes.

'Jackie, please. Don't you think you've said enough? I wish you'd drive on.'

Jackie ignored this plea, drawing deeply on her cigarette and exhaling through her nostrils. Linda, who hated smoking, rolled down her window. After a minute or two Jackie spoke again.

'You don't kid yourself he's in love with you, I hope?'

'No,' Linda answered honestly, 'but I think he likes me. And he wants to be . . . friends.' She spoke the last word uncertainly, and Jackie pounced on it with an unkind laugh.

'Paul doesn't have women ... friends.' She stressed the last word in a cruel imitation of Linda. 'He has women, period, as the Yanks say. Oh, sure, he may want to go to bed with you, but that won't last.' She puffed away furiously. Linda put her head out of the window, because she had begun to feel sick, but Jackie gripped her by the arm and drew her back. 'Look, Linda,' her tone was less disagreeable now, 'I'm trying to save you a lot of pain. I'm sorry if I lost my temper.'

Living at Faversham Court, Linda had got used to Jackie's mercurial changes of mood. Quite possibly she did genuinely regret her loss of control. 'All right, I believe you,' she said wearily. 'Now couldn't we drive on?'

'Not yet.' Jackie stubbed her cigarette out in the overflowing ashtray. 'I feel it would be a kindness to put you in the picture about Paul,' she said slowly, staring straight ahead of her and speaking now in a flat monotonous voice. 'About Paul and Anne, I mean. You know they were lovers once?'

Linda had half suspected it. 'Then why did she marry James?'

Jackie laughed. 'Because she wanted security, of course. A steady type like dear James is a better investment than Paul would ever be, don't you agree?'

'I suppose so,' said Linda with a sigh, feeling very sorry for Paul's nice but dull brother. 'Anyway, that's all in the past, Jackie. It doesn't concern me.'

Again Jackie laughed, this time maliciously. 'Doesn't it? And what if I told you it wasn't in the past? That Anne's still crazy about Paul?'

Remembering Anne's behaviour at Faversham, Linda wasn't going to disagree, so she said nothing. Jackie slanted a quick look at her. 'And Paul of course still wants Anne.'

Linda swallowed and had trouble in speaking. Finally she said, 'I don't believe you. Paul's an honourable man. He'd never try to steal his brother's wife.'

'Wouldn't he? How little you know him! He did it once before.'

'I don't believe you!' Linda cried, near to tears now.

'How you do repeat yourself,' sneered Jackie. 'Oh yes, he had an affair with my dear sister—both before and after she married poor old James. James went on a long trip to New Zealand once and Paul came back to England. It was all very convenient for them. But I suppose he felt guilty about it afterwards, because he took off for Canada. Actually he stayed away from Faversham for years. You can check if you don't believe me. It was only because of his accident that he came back now.'

It all sounded depressingly possible. Could Paul really be as bad as Jackie was making him out to be, for in Linda's eyes such behaviour was unforgivable? And yet—and yet if it had happened it had all been years ago, and perhaps he was sorry now. But Jackie had said that he still wanted Anne. Linda rubbed her hand across her eyes. 'All right, Jackie,' she said quietly, 'I believe you, except for one thing. I don't think Paul's interested in your sister any longer.'

The younger girl shrugged and pulled the driving mirror round, so that she could do her face. 'Think what you like if it'll make you feel any better. But when Paul makes love to you I shouldn't think it'll be much fun, knowing you're only a—a sort of cover.'

'I don't understand,' Linda whispered, feeling suddenly very cold.

'Don't you, Nurse Mannering?' Jackie asked spitefully. 'Paul needs an open affair to cover up his secret one. What do you bet he asks you to move in with him? And makes sure it's public knowledge, so that it reaches James' ears?'

'I won't listen to any more——' Linda fumbled with the door handle, but before she could open it Jackie had switched on the ignition and set the car in motion. She shot away from the kerb dangerously fast, narrowly missing a car coming in the other direction.

'Let me out!' cried Linda, but Jackie paid no attention.

As she turned into a main road she slowed to a safer speed. 'You might just as well let me take you back,' she remarked. 'You'll thank me some day for telling you the truth.'

Too emotionally exhausted for further argument, Linda lay back in her seat and shut her aching eyes. Paul might not love her yet, but he did like her. He did find her attractive. She knew he wasn't putting on an act. Could Jackie possibly be wrong? Or lying for her own ends? That seemed all too probable, and she should never have believed such a distasteful story.

When the car came to a halt in College Street, Linda sat up very straight and turned to look at the younger girl. 'You must think me an awful fool, Jackie. You told me all that, not because you're in the least sorry for me, but because you want to put me off Paul.'

Jackie smiled mockingly. 'Clever girl, to work it out. And you're right, of course. *I* want Paul too. But the difference between you and me is—I don't care what he and Anne have done, or even what they intend doing in the future. Some day I mean to have him.'

Linda jerked the door open and stumbled on to the pavement, white-faced and disgusted by Jackie's vulgarity. 'That's the first honest thing you've said, so now I know you've been lying. Paul may have faults, but he's not a cheat.'

'All men are cheats where women are concerned, if they think they can get away with it,' Jackie retorted, with a cynicism far beyond her years. She had rolled the window down and stuck her head out. 'So you don't believe me, but there's one way to make sure. Ask Paul. Ask him when he last made love to my dear sister. And ask him how he feels about her now!'

# CHAPTER TEN

When the red Mini had roared away Linda walked slowly up the steps into the nurses' home, feeling drained of all emotion. She changed into her uniform mechanically and went on duty reluctantly, unable to show her usual cheerful face to the patients and her fellow nurses. At suppertime the clatter of crockery and the chatter of the patients made her put a hand to her head. The senior staff nurse, who was in charge of the ward in Sister's absence, gave her a sharp look.

'Aren't you well, Mannering?'

'Just a headache, Staff.'

'Bad time to pick,' the other girl said crisply. 'Go and take some aspirins.'

So Linda dissolved a couple of soluble aspirins, and was standing by the kitchen sink when the orthopaedic registrar came in.

'What's wrong with you?' he asked.

She swallowed the unattractive mixture. 'Just a headache,' she repeated.

'You look absolutely awful. You ought to go off duty. He laid a hand on her forehead. 'Feels cool enough.' He stood by her, eyeing her speculatively. 'You haven't been looking your best for some days. I wonder why?'

'I told you why,' she said shortly, for Alan wasn't her favourite young doctor.

He didn't seem to be aware that he was irritating her. 'Man trouble, I expect,' he diagnosed confidently, and added with a grin, 'I'm great at comforting girls on the rebound. Are you free tomorrow evening?'

'No, I'm not, and if I was I wouldn't want your company!' Usually a polite person, Linda was sickened by his conceit. She stalked out of the kitchen and went back to her duties, leaving Alan staring after her with an injured expression.

The demands of the orthopaedic ward kept her from thinking about her own affairs, though they were there at the back of her mind, leaden and depressing. When she came off duty at eight she went straight to her room and lay on her bed, trying to think things out. She was still there when someone banged on her door and called out that she was wanted on the telephone.

Paul's voice sounded warm, attractive and surely sincere. 'I can't wait until tomorrow, sweetheart. You are coming round tonight?'

In spite of her longing to dismiss them as untrue, Jackie's remarks had poisoned her mind, making her reluctant to meet him. 'I'm awfully tired, Paul. I—I think I'll leave it till tomorrow. I have a half day off. I could come round 'after lunch if you would like me to.'

'You can come tomorrow as well. I want to see you tonight——' and when she started to demur he added gently, 'Dear girl, if you're tired take a taxi. I'll pay for it. But please, Linda darling, do come.'

He had never called her darling before and she loved him so much. Weakening, she agreed to come and half an hour later was ringing his bell. He had hopped to the door without using his crutches.

'Do you think you should?' she asked anxiously, and he smiled at the concern in her voice.

'Don't fuss, Nurse Mannering!' He rested a hand on her shoulder and together they made their way into the living-room. 'Thank you for coming,' he added as he lowered himself on to the sofa. 'When I telephoned I didn't mean to put the pressure on. I meant to ask if you felt up to it, but I'm afraid I was a bit selfish, feeling tired of my own company.'

'I'm sure you have lots of other friends you could have invited.'

'But I wanted you.' He slid an arm round her shoulders and drew her into his arms. His kisses were more demanding this time and she returned them eagerly. When he put a hand on her breast she started to tremble and he let her go at once.

'Don't be afraid, Linda. I won't do anything you don't want.' His expression was tender. 'You're so different from the other girls I know. And so very sweet.' He reached out and ran a finger down her cheek to the corner of her mouth. 'I wish to God I was out of this damn plaster,' he said savagely. 'If they take it off next week will you move in with me, darling?'

Linda stiffened, but he wouldn't let her draw away. 'Well?' he asked quietly. 'The idea doesn't appeal?'

She let out a long sigh. He wanted her to live with him, he had called her darling, but he hadn't said one word about loving her. And marriage was most certainly not on his mind, now or in the future. He was being civilised about it and asking her, not trying to sweep her off her feet by his lovemaking. Giving her the chance to say no. And if she did, what then? Would he lose interest? Make the same offer to some other girl?

In a small voice she said, 'It would mean ... telling lies ... deceiving people. I should hate that.'

'Why should you have to tell lies?' He was genuinely puzzled. 'You are allowed to live out as a staff nurse?'

'Yes, of course. The hostel's just convenient.'

'And it matters what people think?'

'Not to you, I suppose.' Her voice shook slightly. 'I expect you've done it all before.' She was thinking about Anne now, and all the other girls that the gossip columnists had mentioned over the years.

Paul took her hand in his, clasping it firmly. 'No, Linda, I haven't. Not in the way you mean. Oh, sure, there have been other women. But you're the first girl I've ever asked to come and live with me.'

That should have comforted her, but it didn't. She swallowed on the lump in her throat and stared away from him, at a painting of the Monaco Grand Prix on the opposite wall. 'My parents would hate it,' she said at last.

'Then why tell them?'

'I'd have to let them know I'd left the nurses' home. And I couldn't pretend I had a place of my own. Besides, they'd be bound to find out.'

He leant back in his corner of the sofa, an irritated expression beginning to appear. 'O.K., little girl, I get the message. You just don't want to come.'

'Paul, I didn't say——'

'Drop it, Linda. Just drop it. I'm sorry I made the suggestion. Shall we have a drink?'

Tears in her eyes she rose from the sofa. 'What would you like? Scotch and soda? Let me get it.'

'Thank you.' His voice was cold and remote.

She walked across to the drinks table, and with her back to him wiped furtively at her cheeks. Paul turned the radio on, and the music of Mozart filled the room. She knew that he was upset and disappointed, puzzled by her reaction to his suggestion. He hadn't expected it after her uninhibited response to his kisses. He had thought that she would jump at the idea.

And so she might have done, in spite of her parents, Linda thought sadly, if only he had said that he loved her. He liked her, he was even fond of her, he found her very attractive physically, but that wasn't enough. He wanted an affair and she wanted something more permanent. But if she did what he wanted, if she gave in, perhaps it might become permanent? Perhap's he might ask her to marry him later?

She bit her lip, knowing that she was daydreaming,

that many many girls had thought along the same lines, and that nearly all of them had been disappointed. The music stopped suddenly.

'How about that drink?' Paul enquired, and she swung round quickly, forgetting that her cheeks were streaked with tears.

She had been standing in front of the drinks table, so deep in thought that she had forgotten why she was there. Biting her lip, she produced a tissue and wiped her face. 'Sorry,' she mumbled, afraid that he was still annoyed with her.

'Cheer up, little one,' he said gently. 'It's not that important,' and he smiled at her, all humour apparently gone.

Perhap's, she thought, with sudden bitterness, it *didn't* matter that much to him what she had decided. It had been a spur of the moment suggestion when he realised how crazy she was about him. Or even—the unpleasant thought snaked into her mind—part of the plan Jackie had mentioned to deceive James. To make his brother think that she was the one and not Anne.

She poured their drinks with a hand that shook slightly, gave him his, and seated herself in the chair on the opposite side of the gas fire.

'Do stop looking so downcast,' Paul said gently, and when she didn't answer, 'I've spoilt things for you, haven't I? It was too soon. I should have waited before I asked you.'

Linda stared down at her glass, reluctant to meet his eyes. Did he really want her for her own sake, or was it just as a cover for an affair with Anne? She would have no peace of mind until she knew the answer.

'Come and sit beside me,' Paul suggested, and when she hesitated, he held out his hand. 'Darling girl, please come. I shan't even kiss you again unless you ask me to!' There was affection and tenderness in his voice. He was looking at her in a way that melted her heart. Suddenly sure that Jackie was either misinformed or deliberately lying, Linda crossed to his side.

She sat down and they stared at each other. She wanted to forget all her doubts in the comfort of his arms, but something held her back. There was something she had to say. To try and explain.

'When you asked me just now——' he tried to interrupt, but she hurried on—'I wasn't upset by the suggestion—it was your reason I wasn't certain about.'

He stared in astonishment, then he started to laugh. 'Funny girl! Why does any man want to live with a woman?'

'For all sorts of reasons, Paul.' She sighed. 'You think I'm inexperienced, but I'm not stupid. And what Jackie told me this afternoon made me feel confused about your reasons.'

She watched his expression change, become guarded and uncertain. 'So Jackie's been making trouble. You know the little idiot fancies herself in love with me?'

'I'm not sure it is just fancy,' Linda retorted. 'Young girls do fall in love with older men.'

He dismissed this remark impatiently. 'We're not discussing Jackie's feelings. What did she say, Linda?'

Something about his voice, some quality of apprehension, of uneasiness in a man who was usually so sure of himself, made Linda feel frightened. She would have liked to draw back, but he wouldn't let her.

He took her by the shoulders and shook her insistently. 'Come on! Tell me! What did she say?'

She moistened dry lips with the tip of her tongue. 'She told me you and Anne were lovers. Is it true, Paul?'

He let her go, almost pushing her away from him, anger and frustration so transforming his face that he looked a different man. 'I could break her neck for that,' he said savagely, 'the spiteful, interfering little bitch!'

She lay back against the cushions, knowing that she had her answer. He was furious because Jackie had told the truth, not because she was lying. She felt exhausted by the depth of her despair, unable to move though she longed to leave.

'So it is true,' she said raggedly. 'Now I understand why you stayed away from Faversham for so long. I understand a whole lot of things about your family that puzzled me in the past.'

Paul drank his whisky in one gulp and slammed the glass down on the table. 'It isn't as simple as you seem to think. I've known Anne a long time, longer even than James has done. I was very young when I first met her. Young and foolish.'

'Not too young to know that some things simply aren't done!' she cried, pushed to the limit by disillusionment and pain.

His eyes sparked with anger. 'What the hell does that mean?'

'A decent man doesn't make love to his brother's wife.'

He looked shocked and horrified. 'Oh, for God's sake!' He rose clumsily and struggled across the room, splashed whisky into a fresh glass and came back to her side. 'Jackie certainly started something,' he said bitterly, 'but you didn't have to believe her. Not all of it, at least. I won't deny that Anne and I had an affair——'

'I don't want to hear any more,' she choked. 'I really don't want to know the horrible details. And if you thought of using me as a cover to fool poor James, it won't do, Paul. You'll have to find yourself another girl.'

She sprang to her feet, snatched up her bag from the armchair opposite and ran from the room, the tears streaming down her face. She thought Paul called after her, but she ran on, across the hall, down the steps and along the road towards the Heath. She wandered aimlessly through the streets skirting the Heath, unconscious of her surroundings, torn by despair, until exhausted and chilled, she found herself by chance outside the Underground station. It was only then that she realised that she had left her coat in Paul's flat.

She couldn't go back for it. She couldn't. Even though it was her one and only good winter coat, and she most certainly couldn't afford a new one this year. She felt that she never wanted to see Paul again. There was no real reason why she should. If he attended Q.C.H. outpatients there was almost no chance of their meeting. Her work was on the wards, in a different part of the huge hospital complex.

Shivering, for it was early December and an unusually cold night, she bought a ticket and entered the lift. She felt numb both physically and mentally, curiously lethargic, as if she was in the early stages of some illness. She sat in the train with her eyes shut and nearly missed her stop. She crossed the road to the nurses' home—and all but walked under a car.

That brought her back to reality with an unpleasant jolt. She apologised in a shaky little voice to the angry driver.

'I'm sorry! I'm sorry! But I—I had b-bad news tonight. I wasn't thinking what I was doing.'

After one look at her white, unhappy face, the driver, who was old enough to be her father, jumped out of his car.

'You poor kid, you look awful! Can I give you a lift somewhere?'

She thanked him but said she had reached her destination. 'I live in the nurses' home. Excuse me, please,' and she mounted the steps as slowly as an old woman, leaving him staring after her with concern on his face.

# CHAPTER ELEVEN

THE next few days were the unhappiest Linda had ever experienced. Christmas was only three weeks away and already the wards were starting to prepare for it, but she found it difficult to join in the mounting anticipation. She went through the motions of nursing because she was well trained and she still cared about her patients, but her ready smile had gone and her step had lost its spring. So marked was the change in her manner and appearance that all her friends noticed it, and attributed it quite correctly to an unhappy love affair.

Angie prescribed lots of dates and dragged Linda out on foursomes with various young men, who quite plainly found her boring.

'It's not enough to look pale and interesting,' Angie reproved her, after one such disastrous expedition. 'Men like a girl who at least pretends to listen to them. You sat there all evening as if you inhabited another world!'

'She does at the moment,' Sue said quietly.

The three staff nurses were in Linda's room, for her friends seemed to feel that she shouldn't be left on her own in her present state of mind. Solitude would have been highly desirable, but they meant well, so Linda had to put up with them.

Angie snorted at Sue's remark. 'So Paul Nicholson turned out to be a heel. There are as good fish in the sea——'

'How did you know it was Paul?' Linda cut in, going even paler than she already was.

Angie gave her a pitying look. 'We're not that thick, love! Who else could it be? He's the only man you've

146

seen much of lately and we know there's no one special at Queen's.'

'There was someone else at Faversham,' Linda said foolishly. 'Tom Bedford. I liked him a lot.'

'There you are, then,' Angie said swiftly. 'You don't mind talking about him, so he's not the one!'

'He said he'd ring me. I expect he's forgotten.'

'Probably been busy. If he does invite you out, Linda, you're to accept. Don't you agree, Sue?'

Sue studied Linda's unhappy face, put an arm round her shoulders and gave her an affectionate squeeze. 'Only if she wants to. I think it's time we went, Angie. She's had more than enough of us.'

Dear, sensible Sue, who didn't need everything clearly spelt out, like the ebullient Angie. After they had gone Linda wrote a letter to her parents, did some washing and went to bed, though not to sleep. Did Paul ever think about her now? Unlikely. He had been furious at her reaction that evening, resentful of her questions, hating the false position into which she had pushed him by her persistence. In her calmer moments she sometimes wondered if she might not have done him a grave injustice. If he might not really have wanted her for her own sake. If he hadn't perhaps finished for ever with Anne. But if that was so then why, why had he looked so guilty and discomfited when she asked him those questions? In her heart she thought she knew the answer. Because he was guilty.

Tom had not forgotten her. Two days later he telephoned to find out if she was free at all at the weekend. She was, so they arranged to meet on the Saturday. Tom picked her up at the nurses' home and they drove to Richmond for lunch. He was his usual cheerful, friendly self, but now and then he would frown as he looked at her, and towards the end of the meal he leant forward over the table.

'Aren't you well, Linda? You look completely flaked out.'

She had put on more make-up than usual, but Tom's professional eye could see behind it. 'I've been a bit . . . off colour. But I'm all right Tom. Truly.'

Later, over coffee, he shocked her by a sudden question about Paul. 'How's he doing, Linda? I thought we might call and see him before the show.'

He was taking her to a new musical that evening. Dismayed, she could only stare at him. What excuse could she possibly make? She didn't want him to know what had happened between her and Paul.

This problem cast a blight over what would otherwise have been a pleasant afternoon. They walked by the river, had tea, then drove back to the centre of London. On the way Linda asked Tom if there would be time after all to visit Paul.

He glanced at his watch. 'Plenty. We can eat after the show.'

'But I have to change.'

'You can change now, then we'll visit Paul and go straight on from his place. He's expecting us around six.'

'Us?' Linda croaked. 'You go on your own, and pick me up on your way back.' She felt sure that Paul would be relieved not to see her.

'Rubbish!' Tom smiled. 'You're a quick-change girl— I remember from the past. Of course you must come. Paul would be most disappointed if you didn't.'

'Why should he be?'

'Because he suggested I bring you,' Tom said easily, and she gave a little gasp, then fell silent.

Was it possible that he was missing her? That he was sorry for what had happened? That she had misjudged him after all?

'All right, I'll come,' she murmured, and had only

one regret—that she would not have long enough to take pains with her appearance.

Recently she had been too unhappy to care. Now, when Tom put her down outside the nurses' home with a smiling, 'Don't be long,' she wished that she had washed her hair more recently. In her bedroom she studied her face gloomily. If Paul had once been attracted to her, what would his reaction be now? Her hair lacked lustre and there were dark shadows under her eyes. She looked rather like someone recovering from a severe illness.

She made up carefully, sprayed her hair to give it body and slipped into the pretty peasant-style dress, which she had bought last month with Christmas in mind. Angie had helped her to choose it and at the time it had seemed just right. Now she wasn't too sure, but there was no time to change again.

She rejoined Tom in a state of mounting apprehension, terrified of making a fool of herself when she saw Paul. Aware that it would have been more sensible to tell Tom at least part of the truth, to have said that she had quarrelled with Paul and that a meeting between them could only be embarrassing. By the time they turned into the road where he lived she was in a state of near panic, and her replies to Tom's remarks became so disjointed that he threw her a quizzical look as he slid the car into a parking place.

'You have got it badly, haven't you?' She looked blank, and he laughed a shade ruefully. 'All right, Linda, if you want to pretend, it's O.K. by me. You're not in the least interested in Paul, are you?'

Tom's jokes were not very subtle. Linda managed a smile and waited while he locked the car. If he chose to think she was behaving oddly because she was excited at the prospect of seeing Paul, then let him. Only it wasn't excitement. It was a sick apprehension, a desperate uncertainty as to how he would behave.

Her legs felt unpleasantly shaky as she climbed the steps to the front door. She grasped the stone balustrade for support while they waited. 'Paul said he had visitors,' Tom remarked, 'but to come just the same.'

He hadn't mentioned this before. Linda felt relieved at the idea, because the more people there were the less conspicuous her own behaviour would be. The front door opened and her hand gripped the balustrade more tightly. It was Anne who stood there, slender and elegant in black, inviting them in graciously as if she was the hostess and not just Paul's sister-in-law.

Bitterly disappointed, deeply uneasy, Linda followed the older woman into the living-room. Paul was sitting in an easy chair with his leg on a footstool, and there was no one else there.

'Forgive me if I don't get up,' he said, smiling and addressing his words to Tom. He looked relaxed, completely at ease, not at all like a man who was under any sort of strain. Linda stared at him, willing him to look at her, and after a few moments he did, a casual glance, neither friendly nor unfriendly. 'Good to see you both,' he said neutrally.

'And good to see you looking so well,' Tom replied.

Linda said nothing. Were they the only visitors, Tom and herself and Anne? Was this Paul's idea of a cruel joke at her expense? Anne dispensed drinks, acting the hostess with practised charm, friendly to Tom, gracious to Linda, who had sat down as far as possible from Paul and was staring intently into the fire.

The other three made the sort of conversation that old friends do make, and at the end of some story about their schooldays Tom said suddenly, 'Sorry, Linda, you can't possibly be interested in that.'

She looked up quickly and her pale cheeks flushed. 'It's all right Tom. I don't mind.'

'You're looking rather ... washed out,' Anne said

sweetly, thereby making Linda only too aware of her unattractive appearance. 'Haven't you been well?'

Linda tried to think of a noncommittal answer, was conscious of Paul staring at her and stumbled over her words.

'I noticed it too,' Tom cut in, sparing her the need to go on. 'She's been working very hard, poor kid. Haven't you, Linda?'

'Yes. Yes, I have.' She was grateful to him for coming to the rescue. 'Tom, don't you think we should go soon? We might have trouble parking.'

He glanced at his watch. 'Another fifteen minutes. I know a place that's never full.'

The telephone rang and Anne went into the hall to answer it. 'It's for me,' she called, which made it plain to Linda that whoever was telephoning had expected her to be at Paul's.

Linda picked up a magazine and pretended to read it. Tom remembered suddenly that he had a book for Paul in the car. As he opened the living-room door Anne's clear, carrying voice could be heard, still talking on the telephone. Linda dug her teeth into her underlip and stared down at the magazine. A clock ticked in the background. A car revved up outside. Paul sat opposite her, saying nothing, but she knew that he was watching her. If only one of the others would come back! If only she could think of something to say.

'When did they take your plaster off?' she asked suddenly, and was mortified by the croakiness of her voice.

'Two days ago,' said Paul with a faint smile, and then she remembered that Tom had already asked that.

'And the X-rays? Sir Charles was pleased with them?'

'Yes. Anne's right, Linda—you don't look well. Are you sure it's just hard work?'

She looked back at him unhappily, wondering why he

even bothered to ask. Did he perhaps have a conscience
about her? Regret that she had fallen in love with him,
when he had nothing to offer in return?

'Please tell me, Linda,' he went on gently, but she
remained silent.

Anne was just finishing her conversation. Any
moment now she would be back in the room. 'I have to
get used to ward work, again,' Linda managed in a
bright unnatural voice. 'Looking after you was dead
easy and I got a bit spoilt. I mustn't grumble, though. It
taught me a lot . . .' She laughed jerkily, saw an expression on his face that she couldn't interpret, and swallowed hard.

They stared at each other in a tense silence. Paul said
quietly, 'Linda, please. Anne and I——' He broke off as
his sister-in-law came back into the room, followed a
few moments later by Tom.

Linda didn't know how she got through the few re-
maining minutes without breaking down. Her face felt
stiff and unnatural, and her voice sounded over-loud to
her own ears.

Anne insisted on seeing them out. 'You sit still, darling,' she urged Paul, so he stayed in his chair by the
fire, raising a hand in casual farewell, and calling after
them that they must come again soon. Anne opened the
door and stood aside to let them pass. For a few seconds
her eyes met Linda's, and a small smug smile appeared
fleetingly on her carefully painted lips. 'Goodbye,' she
said graciously. 'So nice to see you again, Nurse
Mannering, Tom dear,' and she shut the door on them.

The evening with Tom wasn't a success, though Linda
tried hard to behave normally. Perhaps she tried too
hard. When he drove her back to the nurses' home Tom
parked round the corner from College Street, in a quiet
cul-de-sac, and turned in his seat to study her.

'Would it help to talk about it?' he asked gently.

This time she didn't pretend to misunderstand. 'No, Tom, I don't think so. I'm . . . truly sorry that I haven't been better company.'

'Think nothing of it, my dear girl.' His smile was kind, concerned. 'We none of us choose to fall in love. If we did we'd pick more wisely!' His large hand enclosed hers and he gave it a squeeze. 'I could see it coming at Faversham, but I knew there was no future in it.'

'Why, Tom? Because of Anne?'

He looked startled. 'That was over years ago . . . wasn't it?' he added uncertainly, and she gave a deep sigh.

'I don't know. I'm so confused, Tom. I don't know if Paul's still in love with Anne . . . or with some other girl . . . or with nobody. I don't think women mean much to him except just for sex.' The bitterness in her voice made Tom frown, and look at her with a worried expression. She interpreted that look correctly. 'No, we haven't been to bed together. I'm not the sort of girl who has casual affairs.'

'Linda——'

'So that's it, Tom. I've fallen in love with a man who comes from a different world. He likes fast cars and trendy girls. He also expects them to play by his rules——' Her voice wavered and broke. 'I'm sorry. I didn't mean to go on about it. Goodnight, Tom, and thanks for everything.' She gave him a swift kiss on the cheek and got out of the car.

Tom got out too, but he didn't say anything. He watched her climb the steps of the nurses' home and then he turned away. Linda didn't think that she would be seeing him alone again. No man, after all, likes to be second best, and she had made it very plain where her heart lay. She wished now that she had gone home for the weekend. She could have done, but had chosen not to, because she feared the sharp eyes of her parents.

They would know at once that something was wrong. They would worry about her, but they would be unable to help, which would worry them the more. Better to stay away until such time as she had recovered her self-control, if not her happiness. At the moment she had a humiliating tendency to break down at and weep at the most inconvenient times.

There was nothing to get up for on Sunday morning, so she stayed in bed. It was nearly eleven when Angie came bursting into her room, flinging back the curtains and shaking her vigorously by the shoulder. 'Wake up, you dope! There's a visitor for you! He's waiting downstairs.'

Linda stretched and yawned. 'Tom?' she asked doubtfully. She knew that he was spending the whole weekend in London, but he hadn't suggested seeing her again.

'Who's Tom? Oh, that G. P. chap!' Angie giggled. 'Much more exciting! It's Paul Nicholson, you idiot, and do I envy you!' She rolled her eyes exaggeratedly, giggled again and pulled the bedclothes back. 'Get up, and do your best to look glamorous, or I warn you, I shall cut you out!' She danced over to Linda's cupboard, pulled out the fawn corduroy trousers and the Arran sweater. 'You look nice in these. You haven't time for a shower, but for heaven's sake do something to your face!'

Linda got slowly out of bed, completely floored by Paul's arrival. What could he possibly want? Was he just being kind? Taking pity on her because she had looked so unhappy yesterday? 'I don't think I want to see him,' she said jerkily. 'Tell him I'm not well, Angie. Tell him anything you like, but get rid of him.'

'You must be bonkers!' Angie exploded. 'You've been eating your heart out over him for weeks, and now he's here and you don't want to see him.'

Linda sank down on to the bed. 'I saw him last night. That was enough. 'She put her head in her hands and hunched her shoulders. 'I won't see him again. I just can't take any more.'

Angie hesitated for a few moments, then with an unusually sober look on her pretty face, went quietly from the room. Three minutes later she was back, smiling broadly. 'I'm sorry, Linda, but he won't go away. He says he doesn't believe you're ill, and if you don't come down then he'll come up. I told him it was against the rules.'

That brought Linda's head up with a jerk. 'He wouldn't dare!'

'What an idiotic thing to say,' Angie countered. 'Do you think he cares a rap about our rules? He said it was high time you got out of a place that's run like a girls' boarding school!'

Linda ran a distracted hand through her hair. Paul might be indifferent to Home Sister's rules, but she was not. 'Do you really think he'll insist on seeing me?'

'Yes, I do. He's not the sort of man you give the push-off.' Angie's eyes were puzzled as she looked at her friend. 'And why you should want to beats me. So shall I tell him you'll soon be down?'

'I suppose so.' She felt listless, apathetic, convinced that Paul's unexpected visit could only cause her fresh pain. Perhaps he wanted to justify his actions, apologise for hurting her. She dragged a comb through her short brown hair, washed her face, decided, in spite of Angie's strictures, not to bother with make-up and pulled on trousers and sweater. What did it matter how she looked? Paul wasn't interested in her appearance. She crossed to the window and stared out, trying to calm herself down. The December sun shone thinly. There was the familiar faint haze over the trees in the park. She flung the window wide and gasped as the cold air filled her lungs. She inhaled deeply a couple of times, felt better and decided she had to get it over. Whatever Paul had come for, she would soon know.

He was in the small visitors' sitting-room, and because it was morning he was alone apart from Angie. The door was ajar, so they didn't hear Linda enter. They were sitting with their backs to her, and Angie was making light conversation, telling him some story about a recent scrape she had been in. Paul was laughing, his head turned towards the girl, so that Linda could see his profile. She stared at him for a few moments, overwhelmed by love and a desire to touch his face, his hair, to feel his arms around her once again. What a fool she had been to reject him, whatever his reason for wanting her. Perhaps it wasn't too late after all, if only she knew how to handle him.

'This is a surprise,' she said brightly, moving forward and round the backs of their chairs, to stand in front of them.

Paul was sitting with both legs stretched out, the stick he still had to use against the arm of his chair. He looked up at her, his handsome face very serious and unsmiling. Angie bobbed up.

'I'll be off now. Great to have met you, Paul. Don't forget to give him some coffee, Linda.'

Paul's eyes followed Angie's curvaceous figure as it disappeared through the door. 'That's a very attractive little girl. Is she a close friend of yours?'

'Yes, she is.'

'Odd. The attraction of opposites, I suppose.'

'You mean Angie's pretty and vivacious, and I'm ordinary and rather dull?' There was more bitterness in her voice than she realised, and Paul gave her a very hard look.

'What's eating you, Linda? You can't be jealous of that little dolly?'

She sat down in the chair Angie had vacated and her shoulders drooped despondently. 'I never was in the past. But I do envy her ability to laugh at life.' Her lower lip trembled and she caught it between her teeth, praying that she wouldn't break down.

Paul played with his stick for a time, frowning down at the ground, as if he was trying to think what to say. In the end she forestalled him. 'Why have you come?'

He looked up quickly then and his face was unguarded, vulnerable as a boy's. 'Don't you know?' he asked quietly.

She had difficulty in breathing. 'Tell me,' she whispered, and he let out a long sigh.

'I've missed you like hell, little one.'

'You said that the first time I came to your flat.'

'Because it was true.'

She wanted to believe him. He spoke so seriously. He sounded genuine, and why after all should he bother to make it up? 'All right, Paul, so you've missed me.' With one finger she traced the chintz pattern on the arm of her chair. 'Is your offer still open?' He stared and she laughed jerkily. 'Forgotten already? You wanted me to move in with you.'

He lay back in his chair and closed his eyes. 'Linda dear, I told you I was sorry about that. Can't you forget it? Can't we start again?'

She studied his lean, good-looking face, noticing for the first time the lines of strain and fatigue, how tightly his mouth was compressed. He had suffered lately, either physically or mentally, and all her nurses' instincts came to the fore. If he needed her, for whatever reason, she must help him. Perhaps he saw her only as a way of escape from his entanglement with Anne, but even that was better than letting him go out of her life for ever.

She leant forward and took one of his hands in hers. 'Of course we can start again, Paul. If that's really what you want.'

The tension went out of his face and he gave her the smile that always made her heart beat faster. 'Thank you, darling girl. There's one other thing. When you came last night I suppose you thought Anne and I were having a nice cosy session on our own?'

Linda shook her head in distress. 'Please, Paul——'

'Let me finish, Linda. We were waiting for James. He arrived only minutes after you left. I was going to explain, but I didn't have time before Anne came in.'

She believed him, and she was almost sure now that Jackie had deliberately made mischief. Better to be absolutely sure, so that they could put all the unpleasantness behind them. 'Are you still in love with Anne?' she asked quietly, and waited with clenched hands for his reply.

Astonishment, irritation, then anger, crossed his expressive face. 'Dear God, Linda!' he exclaimed, 'what sort of man do you think I am? Would I be making a play for you if I still loved Anne?' His colour had risen and he gave her a furious glare.

'Jackie said that you would,' she answered quietly. 'She said it was a deliberate ploy to fool James.'

He seemed unable to speak, and as the seconds ticked by a blessed relief filled Linda's heart. She should never have believed Jackie, who had her own reasons for making trouble. Hadn't she said that she meant to have Paul, and didn't care how she got him?

'I'm sorry,' she said softly. 'I should have known you weren't like that.' It might have been wiser to ask no more questions, but there was one more fact she needed to know, if she was to have any peace of mind. 'When did you stop loving Anne?'

He shut his eyes again, then spoke slowly, more to himself than to her, like a man reliving a past that hadn't made him very happy. 'I don't remember clearly. Some time in the first years of her marriage, I suppose. James never knew how I felt. He thought we'd had an affair and that I'd tired of it, and he was around to pick up the pieces. He thought I'd behaved badly to Anne. It caused a rift between us which took a long time to heal. Naturally he thought I was the one to break things off, like everyone else.' There was bitterness in his voice now.

'And weren't you?'

He smiled faintly. 'Not that time. I was crazy about Anne.'

Linda remembered the hunger in Anne's eyes when she looked at her brother-in-law at unguarded moments. 'Then I don't understand why she gave you up. She acts as if she still cares.'

He shrugged irritably. 'Dear Anne is one of those women who wants it all ways—the security of a home and husband and a lover on the side. She knew I wasn't planning to marry her, so she made a play for James and he, poor old boy, was completely taken in.'

'And after they were married——?' She hesitated, flushed, and wished she hadn't begun.

Paul's eyes narrowed. 'So that's why you were so upset at my place. You said things I didn't understand at the time. You thought I carried on with Anne after they were married.' His mouth tightened. He shifted his stick with a clatter. 'I'm not exactly flattered at your low opinion of me,' he said drily.

'Oh, Paul,' she answered unhappily, 'I didn't believe it at first, but Jackie swore it was true.'

'And you believed her?' he asked bitterly. 'You never had any doubts?'

'Of course I did.' The tears came into her eyes. 'But it all seemed to fit together so well. And—and you do have quite a reputation where women are concerned.'

She smiled at him mistily, trying very hard to make a joke of it.

Paul was not placated. 'I thought when I first met you that you were the one girl I could always rely on. That you were kind and trusting and completely charitable. That you always saw the best in people. It seems I was wrong.'

He was angry and disappointed by her behaviour, and Linda admitted to herself that he had some justification for feeling like that. 'Please, Paul,' she murmured, 'don't hold it against me. I'm sorry for misjudging you. Won't you forgive me?'

They stared at one another and slowly his angry face softened. 'All right,' he said quietly. 'Shall we forget about it? Talk about something else? Your little friend mentioned coffee. Could you lay some on?'

# CHAPTER TWELVE

THERE was a small kitchen on the ground floor, where the nurses could make coffee for their friends. Linda leant against the work counter, waiting for the kettle to boil, and indulged in happy daydreams. Paul didn't love Anne. He had stopped loving her years ago. True, he had not said he loved *her*, but he had cared enough to come round. He had minded that she had misjudged him. He wanted her as his girl. And perhaps, some day, if she showed how much she loved him, he might tell her that he loved her in return. Or was love a word that his set didn't use any longer? She frowned over that for a moment, then the kettle started to whistle and she made the coffee.

When she returned to the visitors' room she was disappointed to find other people there, two staff nurses whom she knew slightly, and their boy-friends. She couldn't help being amused by the other girls' reaction to Paul. It was plain that they were aware who he was, and they could hardly take their eyes off him. There was some excited whispering, then one of the young men crossed the room.

'Excuse me, but you are Paul Nicholson, aren't you? I'm very keen on Formula One racing.'

Paul, looking irritated, said that he was, but didn't show much interest in the lad's enthusiasm for the sport. 'Drink up, Linda,' he urged, 'and we'll go somewhere else.'

The young man, seeing he wasn't wanted, departed, looking discomfited.

Linda said under her breath, 'You were rather unkind.'

Paul shrugged indifferently. 'If you'd had as much of that sort of thing as I've had ...' He didn't bother to finish. 'I've a suggestion, Linda, if you like the sound of it. Hugh's at a loose end today. Why don't we make up a foursome and drive into the country? Have lunch somewhere decent? Does the idea appeal?'

'A foursome?' she queried, wishing that he had suggested just the two of them. However, she wanted to please him, so she didn't demur.

'Someone for Hugh?' he suggested with a twinkle in his eyes. 'He'd just love that little redhead, if she happens to be free!'

'Angie?' Linda knew a moment's disquiet as she thought of her pretty friend charming not only Hugh, but Paul as well. 'Ye-es. I know she's off duty, but she probably has a date.'

Rather surprisingly Angie didn't, and was delighted to be invited out. 'Would I like to come? You bet! Is this Hugh man as dishy as Paul?'

Linda thought of the quiet, serious Hugh, and hoped Angie wouldn't be disappointed. 'He's ... different,' she said, 'but I think you'll like him.'

Angie grinned. 'That means he's unexciting, but it's on just the same. Paul has enough sex appeal for two.' She must have caught the fleeting look of dismay on Linda's face, for she gave her a friendly thump on the shoulder, 'Idiot! I shan't try to cut you out. I was only joking.'

It was decided that Hugh should pick them up in half an hour, which gave the girls an opportunity to change into something suitable. Aided by Angie, Linda managed to put some sparkle into her appearance, though she was all too conscious that beside her red-headed friend she lacked colour and impact. That Hugh was tremendously impressed by Angie was very obvious. They came down the steps of the nurses' home, one on each side of Paul, hands at the ready to help him if he stumbled, and Hugh, moving forward to meet them, gazed at Angie admiringly.

She sat in front with him, and Linda shared the back seat with Paul. For such a quiet man Hugh seemed to have more to say than usual, and Angie, as always, bubbled with life and laughter. The two in the back were content to listen, to smile at each other occasionally and to exchange the odd word. After the emotional scene in the nurses' home, Linda was happy just to relax, to look out of the window, to savour the delight of Paul's company. When he took her hand in his, entwining their fingers, smiling at her with affection and tenderness, she was deeply moved and smiled back at him with lips that trembled slightly.

He brought his head close to hers and said, low-voiced, 'I know you would have preferred just us. So would I, darling.'

'Then why——'

'Safety in numbers,' he said gravely, and laughed when she blushed. 'Besides, I can't drive.'

They stopped at a famous old inn on the Berkshire border, genuine Tudor, tastefully modernised—the sort of place that Linda's past boy-friends could never have afforded. It was fun being envied by other women. At the table next to theirs two youngish women sat with their middle-aged men. The women were smartly dressed, immaculately coiffured, and bored-looking. The men older, loud-voiced, too hearty. They all called each other darling without much affection and drank a great deal.

Linda had to be persuaded to take a second glass of wine and declined a liqueur, but Angie accepted one with enthusiasm. Always exuberant, alcohol made her effervescent. 'Am I talking too much?' she enquired, flashing her delicious smile at the two men.

Hugh, who was plainly fascinated by her, shook his head gravely. Paul smiled and said softly. 'You liven things up, Angie. You're just what we need.' His eyes lingered on the girl's pretty face, on her full soft mouth and her curvaceous bosom. The smile deepened, and Linda's hands clenched beneath the table.

Paul couldn't—he couldn't prefer Angie to herself. He hadn't known the other girl for more than a few hours. And he had asked Angie as company for Hugh. She tried to tell herself that any man would admire Angie's looks and high spirits. It was stupid to worry, but worry she did, which made her quieter than usual, so that Paul glanced at her once or twice with a query in his eyes.

He suggested that they have coffee in the lounge, which overlooked the back garden and the river. 'Sit by me,' he commanded, patting the sofa beside him, and when Linda did so he put an arm round her shoulders and pulled her close.

'What's wrong?' he asked under his breath. She gave a false bright smile and shrugged carelessly. He stared down at her with a frown. 'Are you annoyed because I asked the others to come?'

'No—yes. Oh, Paul——' She broke off with a sigh, not sure what she felt.

'Silly girl,' he said lovingly. 'There's all the time in the world to be alone. I told you, I'm not going to rush things again.'

The other two were on the far side of the room, examining some old brasses. Paul put a hand behind her head, turned her round to face him and kissed her deeply. Her breath quickened. She gazed at him wide-eyed, and he smiled back at her.

'Don't look at me like that, little one. It'll make me bigheaded!' He drew back just as the others turned round.

Linda felt happier now. Of course Paul found Angie attractive. What man wouldn't? But that didn't mean he was going to make a play for her. She brightened, and began to take more part in the conversation.

Later they walked on the towpath by the river, Angie and Hugh ahead, Paul and Linda following more slowly, because he still moved laboriously. 'Hugh's very smitten,' Paul smiled, watching as his friend helped Angie over a stile. 'I wonder if I've started something.'

'Angie has hordes of boy-friends.'

'With legs like that can you wonder?' he asked lightly, as Angie's skirt lifted well above her knees.

Again Linda was stabbed by frightening jealousy. Paul had never said anything about her legs, which were nearly as good as Angie's. She walked ahead of him and stepped on to the stile, then wondered if he would be able to cope with climbing it.

When she asked what he felt he admitted that he had had enough. She jumped down again and as she landed on the soft earth, he drew her towards him. 'There is something wrong, isn't there? You're unhappy.'

She avoided his eyes and tried to tug her hand free. Hugh and Angie were disappearing round a bend in the path. 'Let's go back, then,' she said breathlessly, but Paul wouldn't let her go. He took her into his arms, leaning against the stile and staring down at her intently.

'What is it, Linda? You were happy enough when we left the inn.' She bit her lip as he put a hand under her chin and forced her head up. Never very patient, he was beginning to look irritated. They stared at each other. Paul said quietly, 'It's Angie who's bothering you, isn't it?' His eyes narrowed at her discomfited look.

Was she so transparent? Would he despise her for such pettiness? She dug her teeth into her underlip and said nothing. Paul stroked her hair lightly. 'Sweetheart,

you don't have much confidence in yourself, do you?
You can't seriously think that I'm interested in that
dizzy little redhead?' He spoke almost contemptuously,
dismissing Angie's charms as of no importance, but
wasn't she just the sort of girl he had gone around with
in the past?

When she said this, stammering over the words, trying
to make him understand, so that he wouldn't be
annoyed with her, he sighed impatiently and put a hand
over her mouth.

'Darling girl, a man would have to be blind not to
admire Angie's looks. But pretty girls are ten a penny. I
prefer you.' He removed his hand and brushed her
mouth with his. 'Have I told you before—you have
beautiful lips. And the softest skin I ever touched.' He
stroked her cheek and she clutched his hand, holding it
against her face.

'I love you so much, Paul. Please be patient with me.
And try to understand that—that——' She couldn't go
on, but he finished for her.

'That you don't completely trust me yet? That you're
not sure how serious I am? Well, I suppose I can't blame
you, and I have only myself to thank.'

They returned slowly to the inn, because Paul seemed
to be tiring, though he wouldn't admit it. Linda felt it
had been a mistake for him to walk by the river, after
so short a time out of plaster. When she asked him how
soon he expected to drive again, he snapped at her,
though he was instantly contrite.

'I'm sorry, my dear, but I prefer not to think about it.
I'm tired of reading in the sports columns what my
chances are of being as good as I was in the past.'

If he returned to racing she would never feel at peace
again. Far worse than the fear of his being attracted to
other women was the thought of another crash. 'I wasn't
talking about racing,' she said hesitantly, 'I meant

ordinary cars. Has Sir Charles said?'

'He's far too cautious to commit himself,' Paul shrugged, and with a very fair imitation of the great man's manner, 'No two patients are the same, my boy. No two tibias mend in the same time.'

Linda laughed and they both relaxed, slipping easily into a happier relationship again. When the others returned they decided to have tea in the same hotel. They chose a table near the fire and lingered on because they were comfortable and happy, until no one else was left in the room.

The girls went to the ladies' room on the way out. 'It's been great today,' Angie enthused, smiling at Linda's reflection in the mirror. 'I certainly envy you, hooking a man like Paul!'

'You make it sound very calculating,' Linda frowned, and added after a moment, 'Don't you like Hugh?'

Angie grinned. 'Of course I like him. Who wouldn't? But with Paul around he seems duller than he really is.'

'Do you think looks are more important than anything else then?' Linda asked, with a faint return of unease, and Angie stared, with dawning comprehension.

'They are if that's all you have, but in Hugh's case— and yours—what's beneath the surface counts more.'

'Well, thanks!' Linda's voice was sharper than usual. 'I know I'm no beauty——'

'And now you're being silly,' Angie cut in, laying a hand on her friend's arm. 'I didn't say you were ugly, you idiot. In fact you're very attractive in a quiet sort of way. Men may date girls like me, but they marry girls like you!'

Linda returned her smile reluctantly. 'I'm sorry. I do know what you mean really. But I don't think——' She hesitated, then decided to go on—'I don't think Paul has marriage in mind.'

'Give him time,' Angie suggested. 'Hugh thinks he should grab you with both hands. He says you're the best thing that's happened to Paul in years.' Though it was flattering to be liked by Hugh, Linda wasn't too keen on the idea of his discussing her with Angie. The other girl rattled on happily, 'He thinks you'll encourage Paul to be more serious. In spite of what the papers say, Paul's not just a playboy, like some of those racing drivers. He has a real future in mechanical engineering. Apparently quite a few racing combines are putting out feelers to see if he's interested in working for them as a designer.'

A safe, secure job without so much travelling! 'That would be wonderful. 'I wish he would accept, stay in London for a time.' Linda smiled to herself at the prospect of Paul close at hand, of evenings spent at his flat, just the two of them, no one else around.

Angie studied her friend's smiling dreamy face a shade doubtfully. 'What I said just now. He does have a serious side, but I'm not sure how deep it goes where women are concerned.'

That brought Linda back to earth with a bang. 'Neither am I,' she admitted with a sigh, 'but I have to find out, Angie. I have to find out.'

They rejoined the two men at the hotel bar. 'You took so long we thought we'd have a quick one,' said Paul. 'What'll it be, girls?'

Angie asked for a gin and tonic, but Linda declined. 'We seem to have done nothing but eat and drink all day!'

She stood beside the others and listened with amusement to Paul's account of a village cricket match, wondering if he would be content to return to less demanding sports. Would he miss the frenetic excitement of the racing circuits, if he had to give up for good? Would he mind being a backroom boy instead of one of the stars?

She couldn't tell, because he was not a man to reveal his deepest feelings.

The foursome who had been at the next table at lunchtime were propping up the bar a short distance away. One of the women, a gleaming blonde with a hard face, stared steadily at Paul. She caught his eye and smiled, but Paul turned away. The blonde looked momentarily put out, but recovered quickly. She said something to her companion, a beefy red-faced man with a loud voice.

'Paul Nicholson?' he boomed. 'Are you sure, darling?'

Linda saw Paul stiffen and frown. 'Drink up,' he said under his breath. 'It's time we went.'

Before they could leave the man tapped Paul on the shoulder. 'Excuse me old, chap, but Chris here swears you're Paul Nicholson.'

Paul moved away and put his glass down on the counter. 'The lady's quite right,' he said carelessly. 'Shall we go, girls?'

He was obviously in a hurry to leave, so Linda started towards the door. Paul slid a hand through Angie's arm. 'Come on, slowcoach!' He grasped his stick with his other hand and they moved towards the exit.

A man who had been sitting alone rose to his feet, looking excited, a young man with a trendy haircut and a ready smile. 'Just a minute, Mr Nicholson. Hold it, will you?'

A camera swung up, a flash bulb exploded, and Paul swore angrily. 'What the hell do you think you're doing, Berry? Waste of good film! I'm no longer news.'

'That's what you think,' the young man countered cockily. His eyes flicked appreciatively over Angie. 'Care to tell me the little lady's name?'

'No, I wouldn't, and if you have any decency you won't publish those pictures. My friends aren't used to publicity.'

Berry's blue eyes sharpened. 'That so, old man? Then perhaps they'll enjoy being important.' He sketched an airy salute and walked out of the hotel, followed more slowly by Linda and Hugh, with Paul muttering angrily behind.

'Do you know him?' Linda asked, and Hugh shrugged.

'He works for one of the shoddiest papers in Flcct Street. Rotten luck bumping into him.'

'I don't believe he'd have noticed us if that damn woman hadn't attracted his attention,' Paul growled.

'Does it matter?' asked Angie, who appeared hugely amused by the whole business. 'Linda and I might quite enjoy seeing ourselves in a newspaper.'

'Not that newspaper,' Paul said shortly, and steadied himself with one hand on the bonnet of Hugh's car. He looked tired and bad-tempered, and Linda thought worriedly that he had done far too much today for a man who had been ill so recently. Hugh backed her up when she urged him to go home to bed.

'I'll see that he does, Linda. O.K. if I drop you girls off first?'

Linda would dearly have loved an evening alone with Paul at his flat, but she knew that his greatest need was to rest. So she promised to telephone him when she came off duty tomorrow, and watched the two men drive away quite happily. It was so different from that other time when they had said goodbye on this same spot, and she had wondered if she would ever see him again. Now she knew that she would, and in less than twenty-four hours.

'Oh, Angie,' she breathed, as they mounted the steps, 'I'm so terribly happy! I've never felt like this in my whole life.'

'Then make the most of it,' Angie advised, adding

with an unusual touch of astringency, 'while it lasts.'

Good advice. This high peak of happiness was followed next day by a trough of despondency. The morning began well, with an exceptionally quiet day for the orthopaedic ward. They were off emergency take and had only the routine operation patients to look after. This was the registrar's day for a ward round, which Sister left to the staff nurse on duty, only Sir Charles' round being important enough for her to take in person.

'You go with Mr Barton,' she told Linda graciously. 'It's time you took more responsibility, Mannering. You've been on this ward quite a time now.'

So Linda accompanied Alan Barton, whom she didn't particularly like, and acquitted herself very creditably. 'Good girl,' he pronounced rather patronisingly. 'Do you think Sister would stand us a cup of coffee?'

Sister, who liked Alan better than Linda did, was quite willing. She sat at her desk while they drank, turning over the pages of a newspaper which someone had left in the office. 'Who reads this rag?' she asked disapprovingly, and the third-year nurse, who had gone on the round with Linda, giggled and admitted it was hers.

Sister tut-tutted and stabbed at the page in front of her with a contemptuous finger. 'Just look at this sort of thing! Gossip and innuendo. No serious news.' She stared down at a photograph, adjusted her spectacles and pursed her lips. 'What an extraordinary thing, Mannering! The girl in this picture looks just like you. And surely that other girl—isn't she one of our nurses too?'

Alan Barton bent forward, then started to laugh. 'Well, I'll be—it is you, Staff, and that's Angie Dennison!' He read out the caption below with huge amusement. 'RACING DRIVER PAUL NICHOLSON AND FRIENDS SPEND A QUIET DAY IN THE

COUNTRY. When I asked Paul to tell me the name of his new redheaded companion he refused to do so. All I can say is, he can certainly pick them!' Alan looked up at Linda, who had gone fiery red. 'Well, well,' he said softly, 'you do surprise me, Staff!'

Sister said tartly, 'So unnecessary. It'll be all round the hospital before the end of the day.'

'Does it matter if it is, Sister?' asked the third-year nurse, wide-eyed and excited. 'I'd just love to be in a gossip column!'

'I'm sure you would, you silly girl,' Sister snapped. 'But Staff Nurse Mannering doesn't look too happy about it.'

Linda said nothing and the matter was dropped, because they had more serious things to discuss, but when she went down to lunch it was the main topic of conversation. Most of the girls were intrigued, amused, even envious, except for a few of the more serious ones, like Sue Baker.

'Do you have to go on and on about it?' she asked. 'Linda's had quite enough, I should think.'

Linda summoned a smile and said that she had, but what really rankled was the assumption that it was Angie who was Paul's girl. Someone had thrust a copy of the paper in front of her, and she had studied it more carefully than she had done in Sister's office. Angie was certainly photogenic! Her wide smile could have graced a toothpaste advertisement. Her curvy figure showed to advantage. Paul had put his arm through hers to hurry her up, because he wanted to get away from the other people at the bar, but the photographer hadn't known that. He had thought that Angie was his new girl-friend.

Hugh and Linda were on the fringe of the picture, and there was no point in denying it. In looks they were most definitely overshadowed by the other pair.

Marianne Littlewood, who had nursed Paul on the

private wing occasionally, commented on this, her expression malicious. 'It wasn't a smart move, Linda, taking Angie out with you! It *was* you who introduced her to Paul Nicholson, wasn't it?' Angie hadn't turned up to lunch and Linda wondered what she was thinking. When the other girl didn't reply Marianne gave her a knowing glance, and added softly, 'That is if you really fancy him yourself.'

When Linda came off duty she telephoned Paul, and asked him if he had seen the newspaper. With a snort of contempt he said that he didn't read complete trash.

'Nor do I, but half the hospital seems to,' Linda said unhappily. 'It's rather unpleasant really. Angie thinks it's very funny, but then everyone assumes that she's cut me out with you.'

There was a short silence the other end. 'Why the hell should they?' Paul snapped.

'Because you're arm in arm with her. And even if you weren't she looks absolutely stunning. So naturally everyone would assume it was her and not me ... wouldn't they?' she ended uncertainly.

This time the silence was longer and when Paul spoke there was an edge to his voice. 'If we're to have any sort of relationship at all, Linda, you have to stop going on like this. Who cares what the papers say? They get it wrong most of the time. What matters is how we feel about each other. So come on round and I'll show you——' his voice softened and she thought that he must be smiling—'in the most conclusive way I can!'

Paul had asked her to pick up some bread on the way, so when she came out of the Underground she went into a bakery. At the front of the shop a few tables were placed in the window, and people were having tea and cakes there. Linda bought rolls and some appetising-looking pastries. As she was paying a clear voice spoke behind her.

'Small world, isn't it? Off duty, Miss Mannering?'

Linda glanced round and saw Fenella Freeman sitting at the end table with another girl, who from her polished looks might also be a model. She hadn't noticed them when she came in.

'Hallo,' she smiled. 'Yes, I have a half day.' She put the packages into her bag and moved towards the door.

'You wouldn't care to join us?' There was something about Fenella's voice that made Linda look at her uneasily. Her face was taut and unsmiling, her manner bordering on the offensive.

'No, thank you. Paul's expecting me.' She moved on towards the door.

Fenella was up in a flash, gripping her by the arm, halting her progress. 'But I want you to join us. I have something to say to you. Paul can wait for five minutes.' Her fingers dug painfully into Linda's arm.

Short of making a scene there was no way of avoiding it, so Linda sat down reluctantly, hoping that Fenella would be brief. The other customers were middle-aged housewives, who seemed totally wrapped up in their own affairs, so if Fenella was unpleasant they probably wouldn't even notice.

'Well?' she asked quietly. 'What do you want to say?'

Fenella smiled then, but disagreeably. 'I saw that picture of Paul and you. Or should I say of Paul and someone and Hugh and you?' Linda was silent, and the other girl, who was as fair as Fenella was dark, moved uneasily in her chair.

'I say, Fen, don't you think we should go?'

'You go!' Fenella retorted rudely. 'I have a whole lot more to say. I didn't introduce you, did I? Nurse Mannering looked after Paul in hospital, then got herself fixed up with a cushy job at his brother's house. Clever of her, wasn't it?'

The blonde girl gave Linda an apologetic look, picked up her shoulder bag, muttered something about being in a terrific rush, and went over to the counter to pay her bill.

'I might as well go too,' Linda said firmly, 'since it's obvious you only want to be disagreeable.'

'You're flaming right, I do,' Fenella retorted sharply. She moved her chair forward, hemming Linda in, so that it would have been difficult to rise in the small space left. 'You weren't quite as clever as you thought, were you?' she sneered. 'Paul seemed to be more interested in that other girl, didn't he? And can you wonder? She has ten times your sex appeal. It comes through, even in that lousy photo.'

'If you'd move, please, Fenella, I want to get up.'

Fenella poured more tea. 'Who is she?'

'A friend of mine. If you don't move I shall shove the table over,' Linda threatened.

'No, you won't, my dear girl. You're the sort who hates a scene. Unwise to take that girl with you, knowing what Paul is like.'

'Paul suggested it. He wanted someone for Hugh.' Linda closed her eyes for a moment, wondering how much longer she must suffer this unpleasantness. 'Fenella, be decent. Break it up. This is absolutely stupid.'

'It's you who's stupid,' Fenella said viciously, but keeping her voice down none the less. Beneath the careful make-up her cheeks were flushed with anger. 'So Paul's expecting you, is he? Has he asked you to stay the night?'

The two girls stared at one another. 'He asked me round for the evening,' Linda said at last.

Fenella laughed harshly. 'It'll end in bed, I can tell you that! It always does with Paul. I hope you're on the pill, sweetie?' The flush had died away now, leaving her

white-faced and almost haggard. She looked dangerously near a complete loss of control, and the thought
flashed through Linda's mind that she was glad there
were other people present. And that was ridiculous!
Fenella would surely not have attacked her physically.
She was a jealous, angry woman, who saw the man she
wanted becoming interested in another girl. She was out
to make all the trouble she could, and it was up to Linda
not to get rattled.

'Have you finished?' she asked, with a calm that surprised herself.

'Not yet.' Fenella leant towards her, and the dark
blue eyes, that made her face so photogenic, were
narrowed disagreeably. 'So all right, Paul fancies
you——'

'Oh? I thought it was Angie a few minutes ago!' An
unwise thing to say, and she regretted her words instantly.

'Is that her name? He probably fancies her too. Paul
likes plenty of variety.' Fenella took out her compact
and studied her face, frowning slightly at what she saw.
'You think I'm being a bitch, don't you, but if you're
sensible you'll pay attention. You're not Paul's type—
you must know that. He wouldn't have looked twice at
you——' Her glance flicked contemptuously over Linda,
taking in the last season's jacket and hand-knitted
sweater. 'If it hadn't been that he was thrown so much
in your company. Very clever of you to capitalise on it,
but you've too much competition—from girls like Angie
and me, and that Italian film star he was running around
with last year.'

Linda wasn't good at handling women like Fenella.
She lacked the killing instinct of some females, but
though she wasn't prepared to match such venom and
vulgarity, common sense came to her rescue. If the
model felt the need to attack her so viciously it must be

because she was frightened. Frightened and unsure of herself.

So she leant back in her chair, gave a little smile and said, 'Do you know something? I think Paul's tired of showy girls like you and Lisa Cantelli. I think he's tired of affairs, maybe even ready to fall in love at last.'

Fenella's mouth dropped open, but no words came. She looked taken aback, furious, but couldn't seem to counter with a convincing reply. 'So if you'll please excuse me,' Linda went on with meticulous politeness,' he *is* expecting me.'

Fenella's nostrils expanded. She was beginning to recover. 'God, you make me sick with your prissy ways! O.K., you may even be right. He may think he's in love with you.' She rose suddenly, drawing back her chair and thankful to be free at last, Linda started to edge past her.

The two girls were so close that they had to touch each other. Fenella's magnificent blue eyes, sparkling with anger, glared into Linda's. 'It won't last,' she said under her breath. 'I give it six months. If you're lucky!'

# CHAPTER THIRTEEN

It was only a short walk to Paul's place. Linda took it slowly, trying to recover her calm, to put Fenella's words out of her mind. She was only partially successful, for she still felt deeply disturbed when she pressed the bell push on Paul's door. He answered promptly, shutting the door and holding her close. She clung to him eagerly, warmed by his kisses and the secure feeling she always had when she was in his arms. For the first few minutes she was swept along by the joy of being with him, of loving him and needing him so desperately that Fenella's spiteful words were blotted from her mind.

However, when Paul drew back and smiling down at her, asked if she was ready for tea, all the doubts returned. While she boiled the kettle and buttered rolls, she wondered whether to tell him. When she was sitting by the fire again she had decided against it.

After a few minutes Paul said suddenly, 'You're very quiet. Tired, my love?'

When he used such endearmeants her heart seemed to turn over, but she wished that just once he would say, 'I love you.'

She regarded him soberly. 'Am I?' she asked quietly. 'Am I your love?'

He laughed, took her free hand and kissed the palm lightly. 'Of course,' he said easily. 'You shouldn't have to ask.'

My love! Darling girl! Just endearments committing him to nothing. 'I love you' would have been a positive statement, which he might not want to make. Fenella's jibes, Angie's uncertainties, pushed Linda into an unwise question.

'I love you so much, Paul,' she said, trying very hard to keep her voice steady, and only partially succeeding. 'It would be awfully nice to hear you say that you loved me in return.'

Nice! What an idiotic word to use, when she felt that her heart would break if he rejected her request. She waited tensely for his reply. And waited, knowing with a terrible certainty that it had been a mistake to ask.

He stared back at her, his face impassive, so that she couldn't tell if he was annoyed or merely embarrassed by her question. 'I shouldn't have asked,' she said forlornly, and turned her head away.

'Linda!' He sighed and pushed a hand through his hair. 'I've told so many girls I've loved them, lightly, casually, that the words seem to have lost their meaning. What I feel for you—it's completely different, and I need different words for it.'

Still she wouldn't look at him, so he moved close again and took her in his arms. 'You're crying,' he said harshly. 'Oh, for God's sake, darling, does it mean so much to you? Can't you tell how I feel without the words?'

She turned to him at last. 'Fenella says it won't last. She gives it six months. If I'm lucky!' She hadn't meant to say anything, but her guard was down and it slipped out.

His hands tightened on her shoulders. 'I see,' he said quietly. 'And when did dear Fenella say that?'

'I met her in the baker's.' There seemed no point in keeping anything back now, and distasteful as it was, talking about the incident relieved her feelings.

Paul listened, tight-lipped. 'God, what bitches women can be!' he said bitterly. 'Why let her get at you, you little idiot? Why didn't you tell her to go to hell?'

She tried to explain how difficult it would have been

without making a scene, but he was too angry to take it in. He quite plainly despised such feminine weakness. He was irritated and contemptuous.

'Women seem to thrive on these petty squabbles. First Jackie, then Fenella. Have I got to spend the rest of my life soothing your ruffled feelings, whenever some damn woman upsets you?'

Hurt by his lack of understanding, Linda said forlornly that none of them would matter if only she was sure that he loved her. Paul rose abruptly, crossed the room and poured himself a drink. Tossed it back and poured himself another. 'Want one?' he asked offhandedly, and when she muttered that she didn't he came and sat down again. He must have risen too precipitately, because he was awkward in his movements and the strained look, that she hadn't seen lately, was back on his face.

At once she was sorry that she had upset him. She felt inconsiderate, self-centred and deeply remorseful. 'I've made you cross,' she sighed. 'I shouldn't have told you about Fenella. Please forgive me.'

'Since it weighs so heavily on your mind,' Paul answered moodily, 'Perhaps it's just as well.' He stared down at his drink. 'I'm beginning to think there's not much future to it after all.' Not much future for them, he meant. There was a tight feeling in Linda's chest. Speechless, she put out a hand, but he drew away. 'I think you'd better go now. You've ruined the evening very effectively.'

She got to her feet on shaky legs, hardly able to believe he could be so cruel. 'If that's what you want,' she managed, and he followed her into the hall, limping quite badly now. 'Does your leg hurt?' she asked timidly, as he took her jacket off the hook.

He handed it too her, then shrugged irritably. 'Just a twinge. Don't fuss, Linda.'

'I wasn't fussing,' she said miserably, unwilling to part from him like this. 'I do care about you, Paul—and about your welfare.'

'Do you?' he asked with cool indifference. He opened the door and a blast of ice-cold air made her shiver and wish that she had worn her thick coat. She hung irresolutely on her heel, hoping against hope that he would change his mind and ask her to stay, shut the door and take her in his arms. He stayed quite still, holding the door open.

'Well . . . goodbye,' she said at last. 'You'll . . . ring me, won't you?' Even to her own ears her voice sounded abjectly pleading.

'Before we meet again we both need to do some hard thinking.'

She stared at him uncertainly. 'About what?'

'Oh, God, Linda! Do I have to spell everything out? You have to stop being so thin-skinned. Learn a little sophistication—or find yourself another man.' He shifted the door a few inches as if anxious for her to go.

'And what do you have to think about?' she asked bitterly, past caring now what she said.

Paul pressed a hand against his left thigh and moved a little, as if he was tired of standing. 'I have to decide whether you mean as much to me as I thought you did,' he answered brutally, and shut the door on her with evident relief.

Linda spent two miserable days waiting for him to telephone, afraid to leave the nurses' home even for a breath of air, in case he rang when she was out and didn't bother to try again. She kept remembering his last words and agonising over them, trying to turn them around so that they sounded less final. 'I have to decide whether you mean as much to me as I thought you did.' So he *had* thought that he cared for her, and now he wasn't sure. And it was all her fault, because she hadn't had the sense to keep that miserable scene with Fenella from him.

Round and round in her head went these unhappy thoughts, endlessly repeated, impossible to forget. On Wednesday evening she suddenly made up her mind to telephone him, and got as far as the callbox in the main hall, when she lost her nerve and put the receiver down again. She had two free days, starting on Thursday. She would go home instead of hanging around waiting for a call that never came, or risking a rebuff by ringing Paul.

Her parents were delighted. 'Such ages since we've seen you, darling,' said her mother. 'We wondered what was happening.'

'Sorry, Mum. I've been . . . rather busy.'

Angie knew that she was going home and she knew why. She had come to Linda's room late on the Wednesday night and found her in tears. She had tried to convince Linda that lovers' tiffs meant nothing. That they soon blew over. Not to waste one more day in mooning about, waiting for Paul to ring. To go round and make it up.

'I'm afraid to, Angie. He was so—so angry and—and sort of scornful about the whole thing. He really couldn't see why I was so upset.'

Angie had been thoughtful, then faintly amused. 'Oh, Linda, you're such an idiot! Can't you see, then? That means it's unimportant except in your mind. Paul loves you and he's furious because you allow these bitchy women to undermine you. Haven't you any faith in him at all?'

'Perhaps I haven't,' Linda said sadly. 'Would you feel sure of a man like Paul?'

'Maybe not,' Angie admitted, 'but I'd do my best to hide it.'

Linda brooded over this conversation on the train

journey home. Had she been at fault? She knew it would have been wiser not to mention her meeting with Fenella. If only she could make it up with Paul, she would try very hard to be the sort of girl he wanted. If . . . but perhaps it was already too late. These thoughts occupied her mind all day, so that she found it difficult to concentrate on her parents' conversation. They looked at her with worried expressions, knowing something was wrong and yet hesitating to ask. It was less than two weeks until Christmas and Mrs Mannering was very busy, making decorations for the church hall, sewing costumes for the children's Nativity play, cooking, organising. For Linda's father, on the other hand, the busiest time was yet to come.

On Friday morning Mrs Mannering had a meeting of the Women's Institute to discuss the Christmas party. 'So you can take your father for a walk,' she suggested. 'You know how he hates these hen sessions!'

The rector looked guilty, and Linda squeezed his arm affectionately. 'Come on then, Dad. It's a lovely day.'

They set out at ten-thirty, crunching along a grassy track that had been used since medieval times. The great red ball of the sun was still quite low in the sky, the grass frost-rimed and the leaves in the hedge brittle. They walked briskly, climbing steadily until they were out of breath. Pausing to look back, Linda saw her father's church, with its squat Norman tower and the famous east window glowing red in the sunlight.

The church and the old stone houses round it had a timeless quality, in spite of the new bungalows on the edge of the village. She felt calmer now, glad that she had come home, more able to accept whatever the future held, even if that future was to be a bleak one.

'You look so sad, darling,' her father said gently. He had come to stand beside her, and was prodding at a patch of ice with his gnarled old walking stick.

'I am sad,' Linda admitted. 'I never knew what un-happiness was like until I fell in love.' She smiled rather shakily at her father. 'That sounds pretty corny, doesn't it, but it's true.'

They walked on slowly and she told him about Paul, not everything, but enough for the rector, who had had a lifetime of parishioners' confidences, to guess the rest. He was a good listener. When Linda had finished he was silent for a long time, tramping beside her along the old cart track. They passed a farm and exchanged greet-ings with the farmer, reached the end of the track and joined the country lane that would take them back to the village.

They were nearly home before he spoke. 'I agree with your friend Angie. It's up to you to make the first move, Linda.'

'Oh, Dad! I'm so afraid he'll rebuff me.'

'Isn't it worth the risk?' her father asked. 'You are quite sure that you really love him?' At her reproachful look he smiled and put a hand on her shoulder, bringing her to a halt. 'I'm not saying the fault was all on your side, but try to understand his point of view. Most men hate emotional scenes—they can't stand bickering women—they don't like having to protest endlessly how devoted they are.' His thin face broke into a reminiscent smile. 'Your mother teases me sometimes—says I never once told her that I loved her, just suggested getting married.'

Linda's answering smile was reluctant. 'But you did ask her. Surely that proved how you felt?'

'Give the young man time,' the rector advised, moving forward again.

Linda fell into pace by his side. She hadn't told her father that the only proposal Paul was likely to make was a repetition of his suggestion that they should live together. Would the rector be deeply shocked if he knew? Or if he guessed how tempted she had been to agree?

They had reached the bottom of the hill now and as they approached the Rectory they saw a long line of cars parked in the drive, some double-banked, one on the edge of the small lawn at the side of the house.

'Women!' snorted the rector, glaring at the damage done to his carefully tended grass. 'Let's creep in the back way, darling, and have a cup of coffee in the kitchen.'

They were sitting at the kitchen table, warming their hands on their mugs, when Mrs Mannering came in to replenish her coffee pots. She put the tray down on the table and stared at her husband and daughter. 'When did you two get back? Shame on you for not coming to say hallo!' She gave Linda a curious half smile. 'You have visitors, dear. They had coffee with the W.I., then I sent them off to look at the church.'

'Visitors?' Linda sighed, not feeling in the mood to meet people. 'I wish you'd just told them I was out.'

'After they'd driven all the way from London?'

Linda stared at her mother and her heart began to pound in her chest. It couldn't be Paul! It must be someone from the hospital, who knew where she lived. She was afraid to ask. Why was her mother's face so amused, so tender, so quizzical in expression?

'Aren't you going to ask who they are, you funny girl?'

The rector looked sharply at his wife. 'Why the mystery, Barbara? Who is it?'

'Two nice young men called Paul Nicholson and Hugh Mansel,' Linda's mother said placidly, turning to the old-fashioned range, where the coffee was keeping hot.

Linda jumped to her feet and rushed to the door, then paused to gasp out a question. 'You did say the church, Mother?'

Mrs Mannering went on pouring with a steady hand. 'Yes darling. I told them our stained glass was quite famous. I thought they'd had enough of the W.I.!'

Linda ran out of the back door and down the garden, to the small gate that gave on to the churchyard. This was the way the rector and his family went to church. She rounded the south side of St Michael's, still running, to the astonishment of two parishioners who were laying flowers on a grave, slowed to a more decorous pace and entered the church porch.

The old oak door with its iron studs was slightly ajar. It creaked as she pushed it. The interior of the church was dim, save where a shaft of sunlight fell across the chancel. Two people stood in the north aisle, looking up at the remains of the medieval wall painting that was her father's greatest pride. Because her eyes had filled with tears, she couldn't distinguish them clearly. She wiped her eyes, and blew her nose furtively. This wasn't the time for crying! She didn't want to annoy Paul all over again.

When she was more composed she moved towards Paul and Hugh, who hadn't yet noticed her. She was nearly on them when Hugh turned round. 'Linda!' he exclaimed, and gave her a welcoming smile.

Paul turned more slowly, manoeuvring himself on his stick. He didn't smile, but as she approached slowly he limped towards her. Suddenly he dropped his stick and held out both hands. Linda walked straight into his arms and put her head on his shoulder, too moved for speech. Hugh went unnoticed from the church. They stood like that for a couple of minutes, not speaking, not moving, then Linda raised her head and looked up at Paul. He was smiling now, his eyes full of love and tenderness.

'Could we sit for a minute, darling? My leg aches.'

She helped him into a pew and sat down beside him.

'How did you know where I lived? What made you come?'

'Angie gave me your address. Why do you think I came?' and leaning towards her he kissed her gently on the cheek.

Her smile was tremulous. 'I'm not sure we ought to do that in church!'

'Depends on the circumstances,' Paul retorted cheerfully. 'Doesn't the priest usually say at the end of the wedding ceremony, "Now you may kiss the bride"?'

Her heart jumped. She was afraid of misunderstanding him.

'You are going to marry me, Linda?' he asked quietly, and she nodded wordlessly. 'Thank heaven for that!' He put his hands on her shoulders, turned her towards him and kissed her again, this time on the mouth.

A scandalised cough came from the back of the church. Old Mr Massey, who had been the verger for thirty years, had come in unnoticed and was standing in the door of the vestry. His wrinkled face was flushed and disapproving, and registered open astonishment when he realised that it was the rector's daughter who was behaving so improperly.

Linda jumped up guiltily, followed more slowly by Paul. 'I—I didn't see you, Mr Massey,' she stammered.

The old man went on staring at her, lips pursed disapprovingly. Paul followed her down the aisle and gave the verger his delightful smile. 'I don't usually kiss girls in church,' he explained quietly, 'but then I've never been engaged before. You're the first person to hear about it, Mr . . . Massey, wasn't it?'

The old man's look of disapproval vanished. He stared from Paul to Linda. 'My, my!' he exclaimed, delighted to have such exciting news to spread around the village. 'Why, Linda dear, I *am* pleased!' He had known her since she was a little girl and had always been fond of her.

Paul slid a hand through her arm and turned towards the church door. 'Goodbye,' he said politely, 'I hope you'll be at our wedding.'

They went slowly across the churchyard and up the garden, not saying much, content just to be together. There were sounds of car doors slamming, the crunch of gravel under tyres. The W.I. meeting appeared to be ending. The woman who had parked on the lawn saw them as they came round the side of the house, and her eyes widened with interest as she noticed the fact that they were arm in arm.

'Good morning!' she breezed. 'Got a few days off, Linda, my dear?' She spoke to Linda, but went on staring at Paul.

Linda remembered that he had had coffee with the members of the W.I., so there was no need to introduce him. This woman was the village gossip, and even worse than Mr Massey. So she smiled and they moved on, only to find that they were surrounded by the other women, emerging from the house.

Someone asked when she was returning to London. Paul answered for her. 'I'm taking her back tonight.' He removed his hand from her arm and slid it round her waist. 'We have to buy a ring tomorrow! How about congratulating me?'

There was an excited burst of conversation, congratulations, queries as to the wedding date, laughter. Mrs Mannering came out to rescue them, or they would have been there for the rest of the morning.

'What made you tell them?' Linda asked as the last member of the W.I. drove off with a crash of gears.

Paul winced at the sound, then laughed. 'Because I felt like it. They're rather a nice bunch, even if their driving is atrocious!'

She would have expected him to sneer at such rural

gatherings. When she said this he gave her an odd look. 'You have some curious misconceptions, my love. I grew up in the country, remember?'

The rector was waiting for them in the sitting-room with Hugh, the best cut glasses on a silver tray. He took one look at his daughter's radiant face and started to pour from a bottle of sherry. 'We must drink to your happiness, darling,' he said fondly.

Linda laughed. 'But, Dad, how did you know he's asked me?'

'Because he told your mother he was going to, and I hardly think you've turned him down!'

The other two had lingered in the hall. Before they came in Hugh said quietly, 'I'm so glad, my dear Linda. Now perhaps Paul will start thinking seriously about his future.'

And a return to racing? Linda's joy was momentarily dimmed, then Hugh went on, his face serious, 'He has told you what Sir Charles said last Monday?' She shook her head and he looked surprised. 'His ankle will be permanently stiff—functional, but not as mobile as it was. And that's the foot he uses on the clutch. He's made the decision. He won't race again.'

Last Monday! Paul had heard only a few hours before she went to his flat. He would presumably have told her, if she hadn't been so preoccupied over the scene with Fenella.

Mrs. Mannering came in with Paul then, her face flushed with excitement, her hair a little untidy. That they liked each other was very apparent. It was surprising how well Paul seemed to fit in at the Rectory. Then she remembered how he had chided her for just such a thought. She did indeed have a lot to learn about him, a great many misconceptions to erase, an apology to make. As the rector started to pour sherry she went to stand beside Paul.

'Hugh's just told me,' she said softly, 'about your quitting as a racing driver. I wish I'd known on Monday, and I wouldn't have gone on about Fenella.'

He put a hand lightly on her shoulder. 'Darling girl, I was more at fault than you. I was very unkind. But let's forget all that! It's over, finished. Let's think about the future.'

The rector put glasses in their hands and the others gathered round, smiling and wishing them well.

It was Hugh who put it best. 'I know you'll be happy,' he said, his expression affectionate as he looked at them both. 'You're so right for each other, though it took you quite a time to realise it!'

# Doctor Nurse Romances

# Accept FOUR BEST-SELLING ROMANCES FREE

You have nothing to lose – and a whole new world of romance to gain. Send this coupon today, and enjoy the novels that have already enthralled thousands of readers!

✂ - - - - - - - - - - - - - - - - - -

**To: Mills & Boon Reader Service,**
   **FREEPOST, PO Box 236, Croydon, Surrey CR9 9EL.**

Please send me, free and without obligation, four Mills & Boon Bestseller Romances, and reserve a Reader Service Subscription for me. If I decide to subscribe I shall, from the beginning of the month following my free parcel of books, receive 4 new books each month for £3.40, post and packing free. If I decide not to subscribe, I shall write to you within 21 days, *but whatever I decide the free books are mine to keep.* I understand that I may cancel my subscription at any time simply by writing to you. I am over 18 years of age.

*Please write in BLOCK CAPITALS*

Name_____

Address_____

_____

_____

_____ Post Code_____

Offer applies in the UK only. Overseas send for details.

**SEND NO MONEY – TAKE NO RISKS**      9D2